Praise for previous titles in the *Control* series by Henrietta Bond

CONTROL FREAK (2010)

... a sincere, simply told, ultra-convincing story that shows what it's like to branch out on your own after a childhood in care.
JACQUELINE WILSON, AUTHOR, *TRACY BEAKER* SERIES

I picked it up thinking, I'll give it five mins, if I don't like it then sod it, but I was gripped from the first page and completed it in two days of my break from work. It rang so true about the system and what it's like to be leaving care... I can't wait for the follow-on book. Definitely recommend to all!
MATT LANGSFORD (AGED 19), CO-CHAIR, WARWICKSHIRE CHILDREN IN CARE COUNCIL

Control Freak gives a realistic insight into the life of a typical care leaver. Young people I have given it to love it... One of the young women I gave my copy to said it was the only book she had ever read cover to cover.
MARTIN HAZLEHURST, NATIONAL MANAGER, NATIONAL CARE ADVISORY SERVICE

Funny, exciting and moving in places, this is a brilliant novel for girls who may be leaving care, or dreaming of the day they may be able to.
FOSTER FAMILIES

A brilliant story, depicting the challenges faced when leaving care while remaining focused upon the potential to succeed possessed by all care leavers. A must-read for anybody working with care leavers, foster carers and care leavers themselves... Remarkable!!
JONNY HOYLE, CARE LEAVER AND CHAIR, BOARD OF TRUSTEES, A NATIONAL VOICE

... fast-paced, sympathetic exploration of the rocky process of growing up.
YOUTH IN MIND

... a very realistic account of what it is like to be in long-term care and the options available once you leave... a good read, written in an easy style.
FOSTER CARE

Powerful, moving and highly recommended.
ON WWW.AMAZON.CO.UK

... an unputdownable account...
BOOKS FOR KEEPS

... extremely entertaining and thought provoking without being contrived.
THE SCHOOL LIBRARIAN

Control Freak is a fast-paced and thoroughly enjoyable story about teenage life and love seen through ... ... gely informative reco... ... falling

into any of the cliché traps... Powerful, moving and highly recommended.
LOUISE DOUGLAS, AUTHOR, *THE SECRETS BETWEEN US*

A fast-paced narrative for teens, *Control Freak* is a gritty rite of passage story for care leavers with characters that really come off the page and happy endings all round!
JANET RICH, CARE LEAVERS FOUNDATION

Control Freak is compelling, and although it deals with some difficult issues it does so without preaching and in a sensitive way. I would recommend this gripping, fast-paced read.
FIRST-TIME TEENAGE READER

Henrietta Bond connects with students personally and the issues that her books deal with are what many teenagers want to discuss. She talks frankly about sensitive issues. Students have been inspired to read the books because of the extracts she read.
LOUISE ALDRIDGE, LEARNING RESOURCES CENTRE MANAGER, QE GIRLS SCHOOL, BARNET

LOSING CONTROL (2012)

When I read Henrietta Bond's first book about Holly Richards and her friends and "family" I was blown away by the freshness and emotional depth of the writing and the story. I didn't think it could get any better, but it has.
L TURNEY, AMAZON

... fast-paced, entertaining and moving, *Losing Control* gives an honest look at the options for young people leaving care.
FOSTER FAMILIES

Highly engaging and entertaining, this book doesn't pull its punches. A must-read for any teen leaving home, and parents and carers too... any young person with experience of the care system will recognise facets of their lives here.
MICA MAY, AMAZON

Gripping, pacey... a must-read for all young adults. Loved it.
IAN PEACOCK, WRITER AND PRESENTER, BBC RADIO

Nothing is overly stated but the tension leading to the conclusion is palpable. I hope young people take the time to read this, especially if they have been involved in or are currently in the care system.
VALERIE JACKSON, CHILDREN WEBMAG

Remote Control

Henrietta Bond

Published by
British Association for Adoption & Fostering
(BAAF)
Saffron House
6–10 Kirby Street
London EC1N 8TS
www.baaf.org.uk

Charity registration 275689 (England and Wales) and SC039337 (Scotland)

British Library Cataloguing in Publication Data
A catalogue record for this book is available from the British Library

ISBN 978 1 907585 81 4

Project management by Miranda Davies, BAAF
Designed by Helen Joubert Design
Cover design Lucia Reed
Typeset by Fravashi Aga
Printed in Great Britain by TJ International Ltd.
Trade distribution by Turnaround Publisher Services, Unit 3, Olympia Trading
Estate, Coburg Road, London N22 6TZ

BAAF is the leading UK-wide membership organisation for all those
concerned with adoption, fostering and child care issues.

Acknowledgements

Huge thanks as ever to my amazing editor Miranda and to Michelle, Jo, Alexandra, Charlie and Shaila, and everyone at BAAF.

I owe a major debt of gratitude to many friends and colleagues in the leaving care field, but especially to all the care leavers, young and not so young, who shared their stories, views and aspirations with me. There are too many to name without the risk of leaving someone out, but this time I want to give special thanks to the highly inspirational Scott King, Yanek Beya-Imhotep, Matt Langford, Jade Aitken, Janet Rich and Sue Hobbs. I also want to mention journalist and broadcaster David Akinsanya, who is an excellent friend and role model to so many care leavers.

Since moving to Yorkshire the list of wonderful people who support me gets even longer. I particularly want to thank Mica May, Hattie Hasan, Eileen Wright, Su Paine, Kiran Narang, Janina Holubecki, Andrea Warman and Wendy Beddows for welcoming me so warmly to the North; and my much-loved "cousin", Louise Clapham, for making me feel like part of the family again. Alison Smith – you get a special thank you because for the first time in my life I can read from my book in public without feeling ashamed of my nails.

I also want to thank my talented writer friends, Louise Douglas, Sarah Wragg, Leigh Chambers, Char March and Anna Turner, for sharing encouragement and inspiration; and Clarinda Cuppage for all the emotional support you've given me during the last couple of years.

Other friends I'd like to include were mentioned in books one and two so I hope they will forgive me for not naming them here. I think you all know who you are and how much I care for each of you but Wilhelm Finger, you get a special thank you because you've always been so incredibly encouraging and I've somehow failed to mention you before.

Caspar, Ewan, Jamie and Michelle – I may only be your "adopted aunt" but you continue to make me extremely proud and I thank you for all your tolerance of a "batty old lady".

Last but absolutely not least – my amazing husband, Frank. I don't know where I'd be without you!

About the author

Henrietta Bond lives in West Yorkshire with her husband Frank, one elderly Persian and a pair of Roborovski hamsters. Her retired horse still lives in North London where Henrietta continues to have various "bases" provided by kind friends.

To earn a living, Henrietta works as a freelance journalist and media consultant specialising in children and family issues. A former press officer for BAAF, since becoming freelance she has worked with Barnardo's, Fostering Network, The Who Cares? Trust, A National Voice and many other children and young people's organisations, and local authorities. She has also written for *The Guardian*, *Community Care*, *Care and Health* and *Children Now*, as well as authoring several BAAF books, including *Control Freak* and *Losing Control*, the first two in this series of three teenage novels on the theme of leaving care.

Note

Remote Control is a work of fiction. The book's characters are the product of the author's imagination and any resemblance to real people, alive or dead, is purely coincidental.

Dedicated to my wonderful friend, Hilary Rock,
whose support means so much to me

My foster dad just rang to say he's won three nights in "Santa Land" just before Christmas. Some kind of staff incentive scheme at work, he told me – after I stopped laughing.

'Not sure why you're finding that quite so funny, Hollybear,' he said, when he got a word in over my guffaws. 'Personally I've always thought I have a very fine future as an elf. The right shape ears maybe?'

Martin's ears are a little bit pointed but apart from that he's about the most un-elflike person I can imagine.

'And what does Jane think about becoming Mrs Elf?' I asked, picturing my plump and very practical foster mum in skimpy green tights and curly red shoes.

'Jane thinks the whole thing is faintly ludicrous,' Martin responded, sadly. 'She keeps asking me why I couldn't have won a week in the Caribbean, somewhere gorgeous in Italy, maybe a weekend in Paris or Barcelona... '

'And why isn't it ... somewhere gorgeous I mean? You work your socks off for that scabby road planning team!'

Martin chuckled. 'Last year the reward for "best employee" was a year's supply of fresh flower arrangements, awarded to some poor woman with the most terrible pollen allergy. So I guess a few days of holiday is a lot better than that.'

'Yeah well, I still think it's cheap,' I told him. 'Nobody wants to go to somewhere freezing like Lapland after a cold wet year like this one.'

But Martin told me that was where I was wrong. 'That's kind of the reason I'm calling you, Hols,' he said, sounding rather hesitant. For one moment I imagined he was about to offer it to me and the boyf for some kind of romantic getaway. Sean has a gig over Christmas, but even if he hadn't I couldn't imagine him getting excited about visiting Santa's secret grotto. Though come to think of it, a sleigh ride, tucked up under a fluffy red rug and me in white earmuffs mightn't be too bad, and those husky dogs do look dead cute.

But apparently that wasn't what Martin had in mind. 'I know you're going to find this hard to believe but it's actually Ryan who is mad keen on going.'

I couldn't believe my ears. 'You mean my too-cool-for-school, couldn't give a damn about anything brat of a brother? You haven't somehow mixed him up with somebody else, somebody human?'

'I know it's hard to believe, Hols. Me and Jane were just as surprised as you are,' my foster dad assured me.

'Look Martin, I know you're used to Ryan and his "little ways" but you're sure he's not winding you up big time?'

Martin sighed. 'Well, to be honest, that's what we thought at first. I mean it never occurred to us he'd want to go. We kind of figured Si would want to go coz he's the right kind of age, and – can you believe this, Hols – there's a "dinosaurs on ice" attraction at Santa's grotto? And you know what Si's like about anything that's been extinct since the Ice Age!'

I knew exactly what Martin was getting at. Si is crazy about dinosaurs. Simon's not a child who makes friends easily coz he lives in a world of his own. He has what they call "special needs", and it's hard to know exactly what makes him tick, but when he does speak it's usually to tell you he's seen a T-Rex on the telly or he's got another Stegosaurus from the toy shop. In fact, I think the last thing he whispered to me – probably about three weeks ago – was that Mrs Stoker's budgie was a "living ancestor" of a dino. Hard to imagine that cute little yellow thing tearing the guts out of a massive horned beastie but I'll take his word for it!

'When Jane told Si he might be able to go to Lapland and see lots of snow and someone dressed like Father Christmas, he pulled this thinking face for a bit and then said, "Father Christmas isn't real coz Mrs Hunter says he's a myth," which really left us none the wiser about his feelings,' Martin explained. 'But then when Jane showed him the bit in the brochure with the skating dinos, he insisted on cutting out the picture and sticking it on his bedroom wall. So that was it. Anyway, as I was saying about Ryan...'

Oh yes, Ryan. That was where this story was meant to be going.

'Anyway, Jane also thought Ryan wasn't serious about the coming with us stuff and mentioned the idea that maybe one of Si's little classmates might like to come along to keep him company... Only for Ryan to go into the most massive sulk... And you know what that's like.'

Yeah, I definitely do. My brother can sulk for England.

'So Jane asked Ryan if he was really serious about coming with us and it seems he was, and still is. He really wants to come to Santa Land. Can you believe that, Hols?'

In a way I can coz me and Ryan didn't do much children's stuff when we were little. We were always looking after Mum, who hated Christmas or anything that made her anxious. Or we were staying in some children's home or foster home – and hard as they tried to make it "fun" for all us kids, Christmas never felt right when you were somewhere you didn't really want to be. Maybe my 16-year-old bruv has decided he wants to do some proper family stuff this festive season.

'So it seems the four of us are going. And this is where you come in, Holly.'

'You want me to dress up as a Christmas tree and carry your bags to the airport?' I inquired, not very helpfully.

'Sounds a great idea, especially the carrying the bags,' Martin said. 'Actually what we had in mind was something a bit less exciting, but there would be a small fee for it. We don't like to take you for granted, Hols.'

My foster carers are dead generous people. They've done loads of kind things for me in the past and I wanted to say no to the money, but it would come in handy and they knew that.

'You want me to feed the cat and the rabbits?' I asked. 'Surely Lucy can do that?'

'Yes... Err, no. Well, this is where it gets a bit complicated. Jane's a bit worried about leaving Lucy alone without someone to keep an eye on her.'

'But she's 18 and a mum! She's got her own baby. She's hardly going to need me to babysit her.'

'Well, erm... the thing is,' Martin dropped his voice confidentially. 'She's not quite herself at the moment. She seems a bit kind of distracted, very grumpy, spending far too much time on her own. I mean she's absolutely brilliant with Ruby, don't get me wrong, Hols.'

I had to agree that Lucy has been a bit odd recently. I mean, she's my best friend in the world but she's just not herself. But when you think of the terrible things that happened last year, it's not surprising. She was crazy about Nathe and apparently they were talking about getting married, and him adopting Ruby and everything. I just don't think she's got her head round the fact he's never coming back. Then having the court case this May and the anniversary of Nathe's murder in August just stirred loads of stuff up for her, and she's been on a real emotional rollercoaster. It's been hard on all of us, but maybe me and Keesh and Ryan are that bit tougher coz we've been through the care system. I don't think poor Si really knows what happened that night coz he seems to live in his little bubble. He just knows his family tried to grab him and he still has nightmares about that bit, but I don't think he remembers Nathe getting stabbed.

Martin continued. 'I mean, we did wonder whether we should leave her. We told her about the Santa trip and we said maybe she and Ruby would like to come with us and we'd get some more tickets. Or maybe we wouldn't go at all, but she got irritated and said she was perfectly capable of being alone with her daughter for a few days. It's not as if we're going away for Christmas Day itself, but we are quite worried about her Hols, if we're completely honest.'

Lucy saw a really nice bereavement counsellor for about six months after Nathe's murder, and then said she didn't want to go any more coz she felt it wasn't really helping. Everyone's been very kind and caring and we've probably wrapped her up in cotton wool between us, but maybe we should've pressurised her a bit more to keep going. I mean you don't get over something like that in a hurry. Maybe you don't ever "get over" it but just learn to live with it as best as you can. I know a bit about that coz of the time it's taken me to come to terms with the fact that my mum isn't really herself any more, that the mum I knew when I was younger has gone. Since she took that overdose in the hospital, her body's still there but the person inside isn't the mum I used to know and love (even though she used to sometimes irritate the hell out of me when I was growing up).

'So we hoped maybe you could kind of keep Lucy company and just, well, just be there. Maybe Sean would like to stop over too, and other friends... You could have a bit of a house party, Hols.'

I laughed. 'Listen to yourself, Martin. You just suggested that a bunch of 19-year-olds party in your house! Don't you watch TV, read the papers? Don't you know what monsters we young people are? We're supposed to invite everyone we know on Facebook, drink all your booze, throw up on your carpets, set the kitchen on fire and drive the neighbours into calling the cops!'

'Oh Hols, I can't imagine you doing that, and even if you did, you'd make sure they all stopped by 11pm and tidied up before they went home!'

I know Martin's teasing me, but once you've got a reputation for being "sensible" it's such a hard thing to shake off, which is probably why it never occurs to J and M to wonder whether maybe I'm the best person to be staying in the house with Lucy. I think maybe they've forgotten that I was there "when it happened". But I'm not going to remind them. Anyway, I'm not frightened of being there. Sean will be fine about keeping me company. He'll be back from uni by then and we can get all loved up. But maybe that will upset Lucy. OMG – this whole thing is just too complicated. It's doing my head in.

'OK,' I tell Martin hurriedly, wanting to change the subject. 'I'll stay in the house while you're away and keep Lucy and Ruby company. Now, Jane tells me that you've got the baking bug off the TV, making some dead good puds and cakes. So when do I get the invite to come and sample your cooking?'

Martin's invited me round for supper on Monday and that's cool because I'm so busy (and broke) that I don't have time to feed myself properly. And Keesh's really busy in the boutique so she's not exactly offering to cook for both of us. It was beans on toast again tonight but there was some Marmite left and that always makes it taste better. Now I'd better turn the light off coz it's way past midnight and I'm due at work by 9am. Night night, world.

It was chaos in the garden centre today. Nobody confessed to ordering a hundred gnomes, one metre high, with nasty smiles painted on their faces. Personally I bet it was Kevin. Probably the last thing he did before he got arrested. Marje still insists her precious boy was "framed" but everybody knows he was guilty as anything for all those sleazy crimes they put him away for. And probably loads more that still haven't come to light. Those gnomes with their evil leers are just the sort of tacky stuff that Sleazebag would go for.

Anyway, me and this spotty lad called Duane (who I guess fancies me coz he blushes every time I go anywhere near him) spent ages trying to find somewhere to store them, while Marje rang the suppliers and tried to find out exactly who had ordered them. She wanted the gnomes taken away but they wouldn't do it, as apparently they were part of some special offer that expired two months ago. If we didn't want them we were very welcome to dump them, but the supplier wasn't giving us a refund. All this Marje told us, very hot and flustered and almost close to tears, coz the man on the other end had called her a 'stupid old bat'. And probably a lot worse but she isn't the sort to use four-letter words in front of "young people" like us.

I got Duane to make Marje a cup of tea while I went and rounded up some of the men and Rhonda, who is stronger than most of the men and 10 times more useful. And between the lot of us – and a bevy of garden trolleys – we managed to stash about 70 gnomes at the back of the main storeroom. But that still left about 30 of the grinning beasties out on the shop floor. As a joke, Rhonda put a cordon around them – like they were celebrities on a red carpet or something. And me and Rhonda started to joke that one of them looked a bit like Simon Cowell on a very bad hair day and another could just about pass for Russell Brand after a zombie attack. Which gave me an idea.

Marje had rallied a bit after the caffeine hit and was making some feeble suggestions about doing a three-for-the-price-of-two offer. But that was daft. Nobody's going to want one hideous gnome, let alone three. Well, not as they stand anyway.

'What about if I customise them?' I suggested. 'You know, make them into a bit of a novelty present. People could buy them as a Secret Santa gift for the office joker. If he's got a moustache or glasses or something I could paint that on, and if he's one of those geeks that wears novelty braces I could paint those, too. I mean I wouldn't do anything nasty, like make any of them really horrible – just kind of funny in an affectionate way. And I'd put big cheeky smiles on all of them, except if someone was very famous for being a real "grumpy old man" kind of person.'

'I don't see that's going to work, luv,' Marje replied, shaking her head. 'I mean, I know you're going to that posh art college next year...'

'Our Holly's got into the best bloody art college in the whole country,' Rhonda informed her boldly. 'You've seen them cards she's done for people's leaving presents, cartoons and whatever...

Bloody brilliant they are! Get the punters to bring in a photo of their nearest and dearest or whoever they want, and Hol will make them a "cheeky" gnome to take home.'

'Cheeky gnomes to take home – yeah, I like that idea,' I said. 'We could use that as the slogan.'

'Well, I don't know.' Marje still looked doubtful, but Rhonda jumped in quick. 'Look Marje, what about if Hols here gives it a go, just the days she works here, and sees if it takes off? Then if nobody wants them, which I bet they will, we try your one for the price of three offer or whatever it was.'

Somehow we got Marje to agree to it, so I'll take my paint stuff in tomorrow. I don't always work at the garden centre on Saturdays coz I've got the café job at my old college and the clothes designing as well – and even I need a bit of time off coz I'm not Superwoman ☺ but at the moment it's getting dead busy and Marje hasn't taken on any extra holiday staff yet. So when someone wants a day off, I often fill in.

After work I rushed home coz I had so much sewing to do. I'm working on this new dress for the masked ball that Davina is having. It's meant to be a thank you party for all her customers, suppliers and friends, but being Davina it's also an opportunity to get a bit of attention and do some publicity for the boutique. She's inviting all the local papers and our regional TV station's been told. Davina has these contacts and she's not afraid to use them. Keesha tells me that she's planning a couple of "surprise guests" – some of her model friends but also somebody famous who's on the telly. It's intended as a surprise for everyone, and she's only going to let on a couple of hours before. Keesh says it's coz Davina doesn't really know that many famous people and can't rely on any of them, but she only said it on the day Davina got her to change the cabinet display about a thousand times, coz she couldn't make her mind up whether blue and green really go together.

Keesh doesn't always like her boss but she does admire her, coz Davina made it big from a really humble start, living in a little back-to-back round here with hundreds of brothers and sisters all sleeping in one room, that kind of stuff, then becoming a successful model and setting up lots of fashion businesses that she's sold on to other people. The boutique is her "retirement" venture – or that's what her rather weedy boyf, Michael, told us. I don't think Davina would like it that he told us that. It's clear enough he's only with her coz she's the one with the money and she's dead generous. However sharp-tongued Davina is, and however much of a temperamental cow she can be, you can never accuse her of being mean. She pays Keesh loads more than all the other boutiques round here pay even their most senior managers, and when she buys my designs she always gives me a decent price for them. Thank heavens for Davina is what I say when another bill comes through the door. A few months ago Keesh and I thought we'd have to give up this place coz we were so broke. Now we can just about get by as long as we're careful.

Which reminds me, I've really got to find a bit more for the Christmas prezzies this year. There's this chuckling teddy I sooooo want to buy for Ruby coz I can't wait to see the look on her little face. And I do want to try and get Sean something nice coz he always gets me something a bit special. And I want to get Ryan this DVD of black and white films of really scary old ghost stories, coz I know he loves anything like that. And J and M always say they don't want anything but they do love their choccies and they have been so brilliant to me. And there's Simon of course. I can't leave Simon out. Last year I bought him a choccie Stegosaurus and he wouldn't eat it coz it was a dinosaur. He left it on the window and the sun came out and then it was a chocolate puddle and he couldn't understand it. Funny how Si's so clever about some things, like remembering all those long dino names, but he doesn't get stuff like melting and freezing. Anyway, this year I'm gonna sew him a T-Rex, and I've seen just the material I want for it.

I need to do some negotiation with Marje. If my idea works out, then I really should get a percentage of the profit, coz it's my idea and those manky gnomes would only be rotting in her storeroom. Yeah, I need to think about that because our Marje isn't exactly generous with the bonuses. We've even got to pay for our staff Christmas dinner this year and we're having it in the garden centre café! Yippee. Not.

And what about Mum? Do I bother with a present for Mum this year? I mean last Christmas me and Ryan took her a prezzie and we did the whole, nice-to-see-you, how-are-you-doing visit and all that. And she did the usual who-are-you, I've-never-seen-you-in-my-life before routine, and she didn't even want to open the present coz she was afraid there was something scary inside. I guess at least she didn't do the shouting and thinking we were some strange people from the government or whoever it is she believes is watching her. That was horrible and Ryan found it so hard. I did too, if I'm honest. But she doesn't seem to shout any more, not the last times we saw her. She's been really quiet, and so thin, even thinner than she used to be. The hospital say she worries that someone is poisoning her food and she hardly touches a mouthful. They've tried everything and they were going to think whether it was maybe OK to force-feed her, but they didn't really want to do that. And I don't blame them. I saw a programme about force-feeding suffragettes and it was so horrible, though I guess they don't force it down people's noses these days. Or do they? I think in the end they put her on a drip for a bit and fed her that way. But can you feed someone like that forever, coz I don't think she's ever going to get better? I wish I could think that but I can't. Sometimes there's no point believing in something when everything tells you that it's not going to happen. You can change your own life but you can't change someone else's, especially when they've got themselves as mixed up in the head as my poor mum.

Now I've made myself dead miserable and that's daft. I need to think about something nice before I turn off the light. And I have lots of nice stuff in my life, like the fact that my lovely boyf's home from uni soon. And I got a text from Ness today to say she's also coming back for Christmas and she's waiting for Marje to let her know what hours she's getting at the garden centre. She's another of those uni bright sparks (doing archaeology) but you can't help liking Ness. She's not big headed or pretentious or anything. She just loves the idea of digging up bones and smashed-up bits of plates and bowls and stuff. When you ask her if that isn't a bit boring she goes all serious and tells you that she thinks it's amazing that we can tell what people had for breakfast back in Roman times, or what disease or injury some Greek bloke died from. Each to their own I suppose. Anyway, Ness says that her girlfriend Bea is going to be coming over for a week after Christmas and I'm dead curious to meet this Bea. Ness is sooooooo crazy about her and I reckon that Ness has pretty good taste. After all, she chose me for a friend, didn't she? LOL.

SATURDAY 26 NOVEMBER

'What will it take to get you to come out with me?' I asked Lucy on the phone tonight.

'Holleeee,' Lucy whined my name in an irritating way, ' I just don't want to come out, OK?'

'Not OK,' I said. 'You're only 18 and you can't spend the rest of your life stuck Indoors. That's not good for you – or Ruby.'

'I do Zumba and stuff on the Wii, so I'm getting plenty of exercise,' Lucy told me defiantly. 'And I use Dad's exercise bike sometimes.'

'Yeah,' I said. 'But that's not fresh air and it's not meeting people. You need proper stimulation for your brain, new ideas and stuff.'

'We've been going to that parents 'n toddlers group that Mum's been nagging on about... And we watch the History Channel and we learn stuff from that,' Lucy replied, stubbornly, and an image flashed into my mind of little Ruby surfing between Teletubbies and programmes about how the Nazis built their tanks.

'Man – or woman – does not live by TV alone,' I replied, hoping I sounded jokey and not too pompous.

'What?' Lucy asked blankly.

'Oh you know, that bit in the Bible where it says "man cannot live by bread alone but by...". I can't remember the next bit but you've got to remember that first bit coz it's always getting used in adverts,' I explained.

'I'm not interested in adverts,' Lucy told me primly, 'They don't persuade me to buy stuff. I make up my own mind.'

'Sure, sure,' I said, hurriedly, trying to get her back to the point. 'Which is why you need to come to the city centre with me, do a bit of Chrissie shopping, get yourself a new party frock... I know your dad will give you the money.'

'Where'm I gonna wear a party frock?' Lucy asked me, but I could see her resistance was starting to come down a little. Lucy used to be the Girl Who Could Shop for England, and she loved nothing more than a totally blingy party frock.

'At a PARTY Lucy-Poocy! Use some imagination, girlfriend! You get loads of invites every year. You know you do.'

'Not this year,' Lucy told me, sounding just a tiny bit sorry for herself.

'Why not?' I found myself asking sharply. 'Is it coz you don't make the effort to stay in touch?'

So many friends made a big effort to support Lucy when Nathe was killed. Many of her year from school had turned up at the funeral and there was standing room only. Then for months after the murder her mates dropped round to visit, but she never seemed that pleased to see them, so after a while they didn't bother any more.

'I've got you, Hols, you're my best mate,' Lucy would say, if I told her off for not making people feel more welcome. It didn't matter that I would say that I also had loads of other friends from school and college, and it's important not to put all your eggs in one basket. Then Lucy would say, 'Are you going to leave me too,

Hols?' which was pathetic, but I understood where she was coming from. I'd say that I had no intention of going anywhere, or getting myself killed or anything. And then she'd start crying about Nathan and I'd get distracted by trying to comfort her. I mean I know it's only 15 months ago, but she can't cry forever or stay indoors all the time. She has to start making some sort of effort, which is why I asked her again why she thought she wouldn't receive any party invites.

'It's not my fault if people aren't having parties,' Lucy responded, with all the maturity of a six-year-old.

'Then all the more reason you and me need to go out,' I insisted, trying not to let my frustration show. 'What about if we grab a pizza and do a bit of Chrissie shopping?'

'I thought you didn't have any money,' Lucy replied. And this was true, but I couldn't let it become another excuse.

'Yeah well, I worked at the garden centre today coz one of the lads wanted a day off...'

I told Lucy how I'd done all the lad's work in the morning and then spent the afternoon getting ready for the Big Gnome Sale. Lucy did laugh a bit when I described the man who had wanted a gnome for his older brother. He'd described his brother in great detail: red-faced, sandy-haired, with a sandy moustache, about 5ft 11 and with a bit of a beer gut, who always wore a green Barbour jacket and mustard-coloured cord trousers. He'd been delighted with the results and told me I was very good at listening to descriptions.

'Well, you are good at listening,' Lucy told me, sounding more like her old self – but then added, 'when you're not being ultra-bossy!'

'Yeah, I guess I am pretty good at listening,' I replied hastily, trying not to rise to the bait, 'but the whole point was that what the man was describing was a total copy of how he looked himself.

Apart from he was wearing green cords. It was really quite bizarre.'

'Yeah, some people have no self-awareness,' Lucy said, a little too pointedly for my liking.

'Look, there's some guys from college having a party next Saturday and it should be really good... they're friends of my friend Dan and they're dead sweet. They live in this really tall house, so there are lots of rooms. You don't have to dance, you can chill and chat, or just hang out.' I babbled away about why Lucy simply had to come with me, because the guys didn't know too many girls and the party would be lopsided and I'd promised I'd take a girlfriend.

'Anyway Lucy-Poocy, I gotta go now, so I'll leave ya to think about what you're gonna wear to that party. Love you – and Ruby!' I disconnected before she could reply.

I'm going out with Keesh tonight so no time to write you properly, Diary. She's got a day off tomorrow coz the part-time lady sometimes works on Mondays. And Keesh is young, free and single again after ditching the DJ boyfriend. I quite liked him and he got Keesha into lots of dead glamorous places, but he could be a bit of a bore. He'd drone on and on about this new remix which nobody had ever heard of, and he was getting really possessive about Keesh. She hates men who are clingy and he'd made it even worse by asking if she'd consider getting engaged. Maybe he thought that after losing her brother, Keesh might want to feel a bit settled, but it's kind of been the opposite with her. She says that Nathe's death has made her realise how short life is, and that you just can't tell what's round the next corner. As soon as she got over the initial shock (which was pretty massive), she decided that it was her duty to live for both of them – her and her dead brother. I think that's a nice idea really, though I can't imagine Nathe ever wanting to party a fraction of the amount that Keesh does. Nathe was more of the go out and do sports or stay home and slob by the telly kind. Maybe that's why Luce has totally lost her passion for partying.

Although I guess becoming a mum slows you down a bit ☺. Lucy used to be the world's biggest party animal before she met Nathe – she gave Keesh a real run for her money. Maybe I should suggest that Keesh, Lucy and me go out together. Perhaps if Luce saw Nathe's sister out and having fun she'd feel more like having a little dance and a drink herself.

Now what am I going to wear? The purple and black dress with black leggings or that funky new green top I got from TK Maxx? Think I'm in a purple mood. But I do love the way that green top makes my eyes stand out. I can't wait for Sean to see me in that. Yeah – I think I'll keep the green top till Sean comes back from uni. I don't want some idiot pouring a glass of red wine down it tonight.

MONDAY 28 NOVEMBER

I was in a teeny bit late for work at the coffee place this morning coz me and Keesh had boogied our little socks off ☺ but nobody seems to care. I guess that's the great thing about working somewhere where most of the staff are students. The manager, Kerry, is a mature student and even she was later than me this morning, and from the look of her she'd been partying rather than studying last night.

There was a line of grumpy looking customers queuing and cursing us and muttering about being late for lectures, but Kerry just said to give everyone a free donut as an apology... and that seemed to please most of them.

My mate Dan was at the end of the queue and once he'd finished messing around tutting and tapping his watch, we had a quick chat. He's fretting again coz he hasn't heard from his girlfriend, Rani, for two days and he's convinced she's found someone new. But he said that when he texted her to ask if everything was alright she'd said that she was focusing on getting a major uni project finished. Being Dan and madly insecure, he wasn't sure whether that was really the case, so I reminded him that he was going out with one of the most ambitious girls I'd ever met. 'What, even more ambitious than you, Hols? What is it with me and all these successful women in my life when I'm just Mr Thick?' I told him the only thing he was thick about was putting himself down all the time.

Dan thinks he's not clever but he's much smarter than he realises, and he's dead grounded and sensible. He was always such a good person to partner with for projects. I'd get excited about all these ideas and want to do loads and loads of research and extra stuff at the last minute. But Dan would say, 'Look, we've done a really good bit of work and enough to get a very decent pass, and staying up for another three hours isn't going to help anyone. Better to get some rest, or we could go for a quick drink and unwind. We'll give a much better presentation if we haven't knackered ourselves.'

Me and Dan did the first two years of college together but he stayed on to do a course in photography, when he realised that he likes the technical stuff as much as the arty stuff. Me, I'm still hanging round the college coz I'm working part-time in the campus café. I've got my place to do Art at Central Saint Martins in London, but they let me defer it for a year because of the court case and me being a bit traumatised and needing some time out and all that. I mean, I don't think I was that traumatised as I'm really as tough as old nails, and I bounce back dead quick from everything... but I suppose I do still get these awful dreams sometimes, when I can see the look on Nathe's face when he was dying. Anyway, it was good that they let me have a year out because I'd have been mad if I'd had to miss a second of my course in London to give evidence against some pond life that doesn't deserve to breathe.

I was also determined to do everything I could to make sure that Nathe got justice. I wasn't scared of giving evidence against those monsters, although the police offered me witness protection, which was kind of reassuring. Killing someone is the most terrible thing you can do because it not only takes someone's life away but it majorly screws up lots of other people's lives as well. I'm not someone who agrees with bringing back the death penalty but I can see why some people feel that if you kill someone you should lose your own life – "an eye for an eye" and all that stuff from the Old Testament.

As it happened, the court case went on for over six weeks because of all the complex legal stuff. The two men who'd tried to take Si were trying to blame each other, and even if one of them wasn't guilty of the murder, the police had to prove that he'd also been involved in the attempted kidnapping and he'd been carrying a weapon, and all the things they have to prove to put someone away for a really long time. And loads of members of Si's family (mums and aunts and sisters and a whole load of completely stupid women who just couldn't get their heads round the fact they were related to violent murderers) insisted on giving evidence to try to prove their men couldn't have been there, when everyone knew they were. In the end, the men both got life, which is better than they deserved in my opinion.

Anyway, I told Dan he shouldn't fret about Rani. That girl may have her irritating ways but she does seem pretty keen on him. Pity really coz I wonder sometimes if he wouldn't be just perfect for our Lucy – when she's ready to think about meeting someone else. But matchmaking never works. The people you think would make an ideal couple just never fancy each other...

Diary, I love my little brother, you know I do, but some days I could happily throttle him. He is so bloody irritating.

'You looking forward to going to Lapland?' I asked him casually over supper at Jane and Martin's this evening. And he glared at me like I'd asked him if he wanted me to chop off his head and serve it on a bed of rice. So I ignored him and asked Simon instead, except you don't really ask Si direct questions coz they can freak him out a bit. So you creep up on the subject sideways and hope you can get him interested. Sometimes he will speak a word or even whisper something to you.

Tonight I was rewarded with one very special word: 'dinosaurs', which made me very glad because if Si goes off dinos before Christmas I'm going to be majorly stuck for a present. He's had the dino craze for a long time now. Maybe he'll never grow out of it, maybe when he's 65 he'll still be happily watching them on telly. Of course we may not have telly when Si is 65. Maybe we'll all be watching pictures projected inside our heads. And maybe there will be computers and stuff that will make it easier for Simon to fit in with the world. Then he won't seem strange any more, coz there will be equipment that will help other people understand what goes on inside his brain and he won't need to speak with words but with thoughts that get translated into pictures. That would be cool. But I wonder sometimes if Simon will even live to be 65. He's such a fragile little boy and I think maybe his body isn't that strong. I want to ask J and M about it, but I know that's not fair. I'd have hated it if they told other people confidential stuff about me – which they would never have done because foster carers aren't supposed to do that. Although they've adopted Si now, so I suppose Jane could tell me and Lucy stuff if she wanted to. But I don't think she would, unless she felt it was really necessary for his safety or something.

Lucy wasn't exactly the life and soul of the party either but I'm kind of getting used to that. She used to chatter away like a toddler but nowadays it's hard to get a word out of her. She spent all the meal focusing on Ruby and making sure she tried little mouthfuls of this and that, mashing things up and fussing all the time about making sure that nothing was likely to make her daughter choke. Lucy's always going on about all these stories she's read on the internet about babies choking to death, and how more toddlers choke to death on meat than any other food, but how squishy things like grapes are really dangerous. And they definitely mustn't have nuts in case they go down the wrong way.

Don't get me wrong, I think it's great that Luce is such a careful mum. I mean it's brilliant that she wants to keep Ruby safe from harm, but she is getting just the tiniest bit obsessed. I think she must have told me 10 times this week that she no longer lets Ruby sleep on the sofa with her coz little kids can die from getting accidentally suffocated by adults. It's a bit like the only thing that Lucy can think about is death. Nathan would have hated that. Sometimes I can almost see him standing behind Lucy's shoulder and giving it a little shake. 'C'mon babes, you gotta be strong for Ruby, girl. You know that life have to go on, and you gotta be part of that, babes.'

That was the sort of person Nathe was – kind, laid back and very caring. He'd been such a sweetheart to Lucy, starting a relationship with her when she was pregnant and taking on the kid of another bloke, and treating them both like they were princesses. It wasn't even like he could pass Ruby off as if she was his – she's the palest-skinned baby you could ever imagine – but I know he'd talked to Lucy about the possibility of maybe adopting Ruby at some point, when she was a bit older. Ruby has never seen her own birth dad which isn't exactly sad in my book, but I guess she's going to be curious about him one day. As far as I know, Mr Wrong (who turned out to be married as well as a really useless lump) moved to Spain shortly after Lucy contacted him to say she was pregnant. He said he didn't want any contact with the baby, and he didn't believe she was his anyway. But he did give Lucy his mum's number before he legged it out the country, so at least there was some way to get in touch with him. Jane said that Lucy ought to try and "keep the doors open", for Ruby's sake. Jane knows a lot of stuff about adopted and fostered kids and how we need to have links with our past, and she helped Lucy get her head round some of it.

Thinking about Nathan always brings a lump to my throat, and I only shared a flat with him for a few weeks. How much Lucy must miss him after she'd been living with him for over a year, I can't begin to imagine. But she still has to make the effort, for Ruby's sake, for Nathan's sake, but most of all for her own.

'Lucy and me are going out on Saturday night,' I announced suddenly, not sure where this was coming from. Lucy glared at me and started to shake her head. But I can be like a bull in a china shop when I've made up my mind.

'That's great,' Jane said, ignoring Lucy's protests. 'It's a long time since you two went anywhere together. It also works very well because the foster carers' support group has been moved this week to combine with the Christmas meal. Although how can anyone be expected to feel festive when it's not even December and there's still so much shopping to be done? But what it means is that I won't be out, so Ruby and I can have some special snuggly-buggly time together. You love being with your granny, don't you Ruby-Dooby?'

'Does that mean that you want me to cook tea that night?' Martin asked.

'If you think you can avoid poisoning the boys,' Jane told him, only half listening as she muttered silly things to her grandchild.

'His cooking's very good. This crumble is great,' I said, helping myself to another spoonful and hoping, if we all kept talking, we could drown out Lucy's protests.

'Yeah, but anyone can make crumble. You get it in packets,' Ryan added.

'Let me assure you, that crumble was made with my own fair

hands. No packets were harmed in the making of this pudding,'
Martin declared.

'God, you think you're so funny, sometimes,' Ryan snapped, so
sharply that I nearly dropped my spoon. I'd heard him being dead
stroppy with his previous foster carers but never heard him lash
out at Martin or Jane like that.

'For heaven's sake, Ryan!' I snapped back at him. 'You're lucky
someone bothers to feed you. If it was me, I'd leave you to starve.'

OK, it was a bit of a stupid thing to say, but I felt really
protective. Protective of my foster dad who'd always been there
for me and made me feel part of the family, and who had then
fostered my brother so he could be close to me and become part of
that family. I hated it when Ryan played up, coz I always felt sort of
responsible, like I'd brought trouble into Jane and Martin's home.

Ryan was now glaring at me. Well, that made two people coz
Lucy was still looking daggers. But amidst all this Jane was still
smiling and cooing at Ruby in her highchair. Everything is water
off a duck's back to Jane. Kids have thrown their dinners at her,
smashed windows, threatened the cat with the bread knife and
Jane has sailed through it all, serene and totally in control. She
doesn't "sweat the small stuff". She kind of just keeps keeping on
and not worrying too much what other people think about her. I
think I get a lot of my confidence from Jane.

Martin is more sensitive. He'd just shrugged at Ryan's comment
coz he has a lot of experience with stroppy teenagers and
understands that some of the time it's best just to let the situation
fizzle out, rather than make a big thing of it. But I could see he was
a tiny bit hurt.

'I want to apologise for my brother's total lack of manners,'
I said and realised immediately I'd done the wrong thing. Why
couldn't I be a bit more like J and M, sometimes? Why do I always
go and say what comes into my head?

'And you can f*** off too!' Ryan snarled at me and shot to his feet, chair clattering to the floor. He stormed out of the room, slamming the door behind him.

I saw the look of terror on Simon's face and wished I'd been a bit more sensitive. One of the reasons Jane and Martin try to keep things calm at mealtimes is that Si has such problems around food, coz of horrible things that happened to him, with his birth family making him swallow paperclips and other stuff.

'Sorry,' I apologised, immediately. At least I was ready to admit my mistakes. 'That was pretty stupid of me. I've made it worse.'

Martin put out a hand and circled his fingers around Si's wrist. This was something Si really liked. He wasn't a kid you could really hug or put an arm round but he responded to little gestures like that. I put out a hand too and Si moved his free hand to rest his fingertips against mine. We have this bond, me and Si, ever since we had this time together in the kitchen when he first moved in and I made him a milkshake.

'Maybe not the ideal response, Holly, but it's OK,' Jane said, being very tactful, but never taking her eyes off Ruby, who was reaching out her sturdy little fingers to grasp the toy dog that Jane was showing her. 'Teenage boys are from another planet and we haven't yet found the manual to unscramble them.'

Jane's knowledge of technology is back in the Dark Ages, but I understood what she was trying to say.

'Yeah, it would be good if you could put teenage boys on "Pause" – for as long as you needed to,' I told Jane.

'I think you need to get a grip, Holly,' Lucy spoke out suddenly. 'All you do is tell other people what to do. You need to stop and look at yourself and stop being such a total control freak.'

In all the years, my friend and foster sister had never spoken to me like that. I was utterly gobsmacked.

'OK, Hollybear, give me a hand with the washing up,' Martin

said suddenly. I jumped up to join him, conscious that I could feel tears pricking in my eyes.

In the kitchen Martin gave me a hug. 'Living in this house is like living with a lot of bears with sore heads,' Martin explained kindly, 'You get used to it after a while, Hols. Sometimes it feels like you can't do anything right for anyone.'

'Yeah, but I really want to help Lucy. I wasn't getting at her or anything,' I sniffled into Martin's shoulder. 'She just really seems to hate me at the moment.'

'She's been strange with all of us, if that's any consolation,' Martin told me. 'Even Jane doesn't quite know what to do with her. Since she stopped crying all the time she's just got more moody and withdrawn. I almost wish she'd go back to the crying because at least you felt there was something you could do, even if it was just sitting with her and holding her hand.'

It must be so hard for him. Lucy's always been the apple of his eye and she was a real "Daddy's girl". She'd pushed him away even worse than she'd treated me lately.

'And Ryan's just being 16,' Martin continued. 'You know what some boys are like. Can't quite put into words what they really want to say...'

Ryan has always been a difficult brother to fathom out. He's done some pretty aggravating stuff when he's got into a muddle with his feelings. I guess I should be used to him by now.

'What were you like? I mean at his age?' I asked. It was hard to imagine that Martin hasn't been middle-aged and kind and sensible for his whole life.

'I was spotty, very spotty,' he said, smiling. 'And for years I couldn't speak to girls or other boys. Or parents, or teachers or... well anyone really, except my dog. Until I was at least 25... maybe 35. I used to tell my dog a lot of things.'

'What kind of dog?' I asked, surprised that I'd never heard

Martin mention his dog before.

'It was a collie cross – though nobody really knew what it was crossed with. Probably something with a bit of poodle in it, and a bit of dachshund and a bit of greyhound – and probably a bit of terrier. Oh, and a bit of St Bernard. Other than that it was a pretty normal kind of dog.'

'So what did you call it, this totally weird dog?'

'Bob.'

'Highly original!'

'Yes, wasn't it? An original name for a very original dog.'

'But what did you say to this Bob?'

'Oh, I told him everything. About how Mrs Calloway was mean to me because I was terrible at French verbs, about how the girl I fancied was going out with the boy who bullied me, about how my parents didn't understand me because... well, because nobody understood me, and about how I was going to be a poet or a musician when I grew up.'

Martin works in town planning and I can't imagine him doing anything else. It's hard to picture my portly, balding foster father jammin' with a spliff in his hand.

'You wanted to be a poet or a musician? Weren't they all weird and into drugs and flower power stuff back then?'

'Well, I'm not quite that old, Hollybear, but I guess I was a sort of hippy when hippies were definitely out of fashion... But yes, I did want to do something that would really get up the noses of my parents. My dad thought all poets were pathetic, and he used to rant at the television when *Top of the Pops* came on.'

'I think Ryan could be a poet,' I told Martin. 'He could be one of those angry ones who do that performance stuff.'

'Isn't that called "rapping"?' Martin asked, playing the innocent.

I raised my eyebrows at him. 'I thought you said you weren't that old… but now I'm beginning to wonder… '

'I know nothing,' Martin replied, with a twinkle in his eye. 'But I think you're right, Holly. Your brother has a lot inside him that he needs to express. Perhaps he needs a dog called Bob to tell it all to.'

'Would Jane allow a dog?' I asked. Then I realised that Martin wasn't being totally serious. 'But honestly, a dog might be a good idea… though what about Boots?'

'Boots is a very old and very wise cat. He would soon put a dog in its place. And I don't think Jane would mind a dog. She's always liked them. But do you think it's what Ryan really needs?'

I love it that Martin always asks my opinion about my brother. Lots of adults treat young people like we know nothing at all, especially when it comes to our own family.

'I don't think Ryan knows what Ryan needs at the moment, but I guess you could ask him about a dog,' I told Martin.

'Well, it wouldn't hurt to have a bit of a conversation with him. After all, he can only tell me I'm not as funny as I think I am, which I already know,' Martin grimaced. 'And I'm a tough old stick really and can take a lot of knocks.'

I told Martin that yes, he was pretty tough and he would be brilliant at getting Ryan to talk. But that isn't really true. Martin just is… well, he's just Martin, and sometimes that's all he needs to be. Most kids talk to him in the end, not because of anything he does or says, just because he's solid and comfortable and someone you can trust 100 per cent.

'And Lucy will be OK as well, Hols,' Martin reassured me. 'You'll see, she'll be on that phone tomorrow and saying she's sorry.'

I hope Martin is right. It was hard saying goodbye to everyone with my BF/foster sister ignoring me and my brother barricaded behind his bedroom door. But I texted them both on the way home to wish them a good night and send a hug.

Martin said it was far too cold and he wouldn't hear of me taking the bus, so he gave me a lift to the flat. We didn't speak much on the drive and he played some strange music in the car and said it was called *Dark Side of the Moon* or something. It just sounded like a lot of strange noise to me. I imagine maybe Sean would quite like it. I must ask if he's ever heard of it.

TUESDAY 29 NOVEMBER

9.45pm

I'm having an early night coz I've got an early start.

Result! Lucy texted to say she was sorry she'd been narky with me, and maybe she would come to the party on Saturday. I wonder if Jane had a chat with her after I left. I hope not, as I'd like to think she got to realise that all on her own. Anyway, Luce is thinking about coming out with me and that's what matters.

My brother, however, has still not been in touch. But I guess that's not so unusual and I'm bored of worrying about him. He lives with Martin and Jane and they are the World's Most Sensible People. They were great foster carers to me and I trusted them more than any other adults I knew to look after my brother. I guess I never trusted my mum to care for me or Ryan. I knew she loved us – and she probably still does – but she wasn't very good at the motherly stuff, even when we were little. Even back then she was always thinking about other things, like whether the people across the road were spying on us or whether the white van man was really someone from the council checking up on whether she'd paid our council tax. She was always fretting about something. I guess it was no wonder she couldn't think much about whether we had clean clothes for school or enough food on the table. I was always having to remind her or get Dad to do it instead. (If Dad was living there and hadn't moved out coz he couldn't take any more of Mum's craziness.) Sometimes when Mum was really bad, she'd just stay in bed for days and say she was too scared to go out. When that happened and I was really little I got laughed at for being a bit smelly when I was in primary school, and I hated that, so I soon learned how to do stuff like wash my own hair and put on the washing machine. I did the same stuff for my brother. I even used to bathe him and dress him myself, and I walked him to school. I made him wait for me in the playground at the end of the day so he didn't have to walk home alone. Sometimes I wonder if it would've been better if I hadn't, then maybe the school or social services would've realised that Mum was struggling.

Jane says I shouldn't think like that. She says that I shouldn't ever blame myself for anything that happened when I was a kid because kids aren't born to look after adults. I guess she's right but I still feel bad about it. Jane's pretty clued up about mental health stuff; she has this older sister who got a lot of depression when she was growing up.

I said I wasn't going to write much coz I need my beauty sleep and here I am going on about Mum and Ryan. Jane would tell me that sometimes I need to put all my responsibilities in an envelope and post them back to her, so she can look after them for me. 'Go and be a young woman, Hols,' she says. 'You spent too much of your childhood being a mum. Now it's your time to have fun.'

I know Jane is right. I wouldn't want to be like Lucy and have all that responsibility. I mean Ruby is dead cute to cuddle and play with, but I wouldn't want to be a mum full time. Not yet anyway. I think it's wrong that the papers and telly are always slagging off "teenage mums" coz some young mums are brilliant, but that doesn't mean it's right for everybody. Lucy always wanted kids so when she knew she was pregnant she wouldn't even consider having an abortion or giving up that baby. But some girls aren't ready for that, and they should have choices. Bringing a life into the world is a massive responsibility and you've got to be ready for it, otherwise you screw up someone else's life as well as your own.

Listen to me! I need to have my own show on the radio or telly – like those American channels where people just spout on and on about what they believe without worrying what other people think. Having your own opinions is good, but that doesn't mean you have to tell other people what they should or shouldn't think. You need to know your own mind but you've got to recognise that other people have their own minds too, and you can't brainwash them into thinking stuff they don't want to think.

There I go again. Enough!!!!!!! I AM GOING TO TURN OUT THE LIGHT.

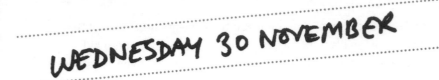

WEDNESDAY 30 NOVEMBER

Such a brilliant day! Keesh and I got the early train down to London, courtesy of Davina. Davina needed someone to take some clothes to a magazine that wants them for a fashion shoot and she also needed a few of her favourite bits and pieces brought back from the city – a lipstick she can only get from this special shop in Covent Garden and this coffee from Harrods. And she needed Keesh to drop off a few early Chrissie presents to some of her special friends, all of which meant quite a lot of stuff to carry. So Keesh said what if I went too and Davina said, 'Perfect,' and being a nice woman at heart, she paid some ridiculous amount for me and Keesh to travel first class. We had brekkie on the train and you could order whatever you liked and have refills of as much tea and coffee as you wanted. And there were proper linen tablecloths and fancy linen napkins, and the waiter fussed over us coz we were young and pretty and a lot nicer than some of the grumpy passengers he had to deal with. 'I think that's whatsisface, that MP who got into big trouble coz he fiddled his expenses,' Keesh whispered, waving a perfectly manicured hand at some scowling man in a business suit, sitting a couple of sections down from us.

She might have been right but I've never been good at faces.

I could get used to being treated like that. Of course, Davina said it was coz she didn't want any of her precious items getting crushed on the journey, but honestly I think it cost her more than a courier company would've done. I think she wanted to say thank you to Keesh for all her hard work, and I know she really likes the clothes I make for her.

Doing the deliveries was fun. We got sent up to the 20th floor of a really cool glass building where the mag is based. The fashion editor wasn't in but she'd left instructions with her assistant that we had to be looked after properly coz we worked for her old friend Davina. So they'd got in really nice pastries and yummy donuts for us. We were still stuffed with bacon and egg and all that toast from the train, but it would've been rude to say no ☺. We ate them in this little seating area with really cool leather chairs and a table – all in white. And we had this amazing view of the whole of London. The river really does look like it does on *EastEnders* – like a ribbon that twists and winds. We could see the London Eye and the Houses of Parliament and the assistant, who was this dead nice gay guy called Carlton, showed us where to look to see St Paul's Cathedral and the Tower of London, and he told us where to get the best cocktails in the city.

Next we took a taxi to Knightsbridge and dropped off a great big package (which Keesh told me was a gorgeous handbag) to this tiny little office where the secretary gave us a parcel to take back to Davina. I think it was a piece of jewellery or something. Then we got a cab on to Camden and took the second parcel (a vase, I think) into a cute little bookshop where the guy looked a bit like the picture of Charles Dickens on my school copy of *Great Expectations*. He had one of those fancy waistcoats and a huge pocket watch and this silk scarf thing round his neck (think they call them cravats). He said that he'd make sure that his wife got

Davina's present. He told us that Davina and his wife had been to the same school.

We went into the market in Camden and it was totally amazing. Sooooo many shops and such fab stuff. There's lots of vintage and goth and emo and punk, and there's second-hand stuff as well as dead expensive new clothes. There are places where you can get brilliantly designed cheap T-shirts and places where the clothes cost even more than Davina's. There's beautiful silver jewellery and pottery and furniture and cushions and rugs and carpets from all over the world. You can pick up retro Sixties stuff or really antique things, or some pretty cutting-edge objects that look like they've been imported from Scandinavia. Me and Keesh didn't really have any spare money but I bought a little painted box that really caught Keesh's eye. She went off to look at something else and I managed to buy it when she wasn't around. I think she'll be thrilled when she gets it for Christmas.

And then we met my lovely boyf. We'd arranged to meet him by the Regent's Canal which runs through the middle of Camden. (Me and Keesh were late, of course, coz Keesh just had to try on this fabulous floaty dress in pink and orange swirls, and I took a sneaky pic, so we can make something similar for her when I get a chance to tie-dye some material.) He was waiting, stamping his feet in the cold and with his hands tucked under his elbows, and his shoulders all hunched up, coz like most men he never manages to wear enough warm things for the weather. His hair was all fluffed up and a bit spiky and he was smiling when he saw me. My heart did a small kind of jump in my ribcage. It's only been a few weeks but it feels like forever.

Keesh was brilliant and said she wanted to go and do a bit of shopping on her own before meeting up with her friend Mel, who works near Oxford Street. But me and Sean said that she must at least stay and have something to eat. There were loads of places, from posh restaurants to little cafés and stalls that sold takeaway snacks. We found a café that did Turkish food and we had this delicious lamb and peppers and couscous dish, sitting at orange plastic tables overlooking the street. It was fun watching the world go by. There were plenty of young people like us, and people who looked like they were doing some early Christmas shopping, but there were also tourists from all over the world and some of the traders and stallholders have probably worked there for years.

Me and Sean had planned to go to the zoo for the afternoon but it was so cold that we had second thoughts. It's also dead expensive to get in. We decided to get the tube and visit the National Portrait Gallery. We've done most of the big museums and galleries since he's been in London, but I haven't seen the portrait gallery. We don't exactly like the same things but we made time to see each other's favourite stuff. Sean is really into history and people he's read about – and written songs about – and he wanted to see the paintings of Henry VIII and Anne Boleyn and other people from that time, like Thomas Moore. He also wanted to see the romantic poet, Byron, and the poet, Sylvia Plath (such a sad story, she killed herself) and I wanted to see some of the early 20th-century painters we'd studied at college and a painting of Emmeline Pankhurst, simply coz she's a famous suffragette who helped get us women the vote. I love going to places like that with Sean; we talk a lot about what we see – not clever stuff like some people who just spout out all the facts – but how it makes us feel. I told Sean that I think I'd be so proud if I could paint a picture that really captured the "soul" of someone, so that everyone who looked at it instantly knew who it was, even if it was an abstract kind of painting. He said he understood that and he was sure that one day I'd manage it because I was so talented and I worked so hard on my art. He told me about some artist he'd heard of who paints people's auras, what they're like inside their heads, and he'd seen a picture of his friend's dad's aura and it was a bit like a thermal image showing all these oranges and reds and blue patches, and some really dark colours. I asked him what that meant and he said he didn't have a clue – and we laughed because it was silly and funny. But you're not really supposed to laugh or talk loudly in galleries and some people turned round to stare at us. So I kissed my boyfriend there, right in front of all those people, and right in front of a rather stern painting of Winston Churchill. I don't know who looked most disapproving.

Then we snuck back to Sean's room at college just for a little bit and I wondered how I'd managed without my lovely man for so long. Afterwards I curled up in his arms and he kissed my bare shoulders and told me he loves me more and more every time he sees me, and I said that was adorable, and I knew what he meant because I felt the same.

'We're going to have such a good time together while my lot are in Lapland,' I told him. 'Just you and me and a cat and two bunnies.'

'And don't forget Lucy,' Sean said. 'Although from what you say, I don't think she's going to want to spend much time with us.'

'Yeah, poor Lucy. It's so not fair,' I said and I meant it. When I'm with Sean like this I realise how much it must hurt that Nathan is never going to hold her again.

We met Keesh at the platform at Euston and Mel was with her. I hadn't seen her since Nathe's funeral. Mel and me never got on that brilliantly coz I think we were both a teeny bit jealous about Keesh's friendship. And there was this thing about her once fancying my ex-boyfriend, Tol, and being a bit funny when we got together, but that was a very long time ago. We're older now. Anyway, Mel was in care too and that kind of creates a bond (unless someone is really horrible), so we all had a drink together at this rather boring bar in the station. Mel looked amazing, like she always did. She still has spiky hair but it's reddish orange these days and she's had her nose pierced. She's not working at the moment coz the clothes place she worked in laid off several of their staff. She's been doing a bit of shift work in what sounds like a sweat shop and I think she's sleeping on a friend's sofa. She wouldn't say much about it and I got the feeling she's embarrassed and a bit worried. Mel was always so confident about her future, but I think it's maybe just a blip and she'll soon come back fighting. Instead she had lots of questions to ask Sean about The Static. It seems she's a fan and saw the band a couple of months back. Sean said that next time she should come backstage and say hello, and she said that would be cool. I know he's only being friendly, but Mel has the most amazing pale skin and she is pretty gorgeous. But I'm not like that any more, I trust my boyf and I know he trusts me. We've had our moments and we've both been unfaithful but we promised each other we would always be honest in future. And I'm certainly sticking to my side of the bargain.

The train was packed on the way back and it felt sooooo cool shimmying into our first-class seats, past all those stressed out looking commuters with their bags and briefcases. Lots of them had to stand up for the first part of the journey and I did feel a teeny bit guilty. But then loads of people got off at the first stop and the train seemed to let out a sigh of relief and everyone found seats.

Me and Keesh ate and drank as much free food as we could on the way back. We're both saving so hard for Christmas that we may have to live on cornflakes for the next couple of weeks, so it's good to stock up.

I got a text from my brother this morning. He sounded pretty pissed off. He had a visit planned with Susanna at the weekend and it's been cancelled coz she's got flu, 'or so she sez,' Ryan informed me.

I texted back to say that loads of people have flu and our manager, Kerry, didn't turn up at the café today coz she was poorly. And anyway, Susanna wasn't the kind of person to cancel without a very good reason. I told Ryan:

I bet she will come and see you soon as shez betta

He texted back to say: *Yeah. Very likely.* So I could tell he was really upset.

Susanna appeared a year ago. She is Ryan's half-sister. Me and Ryan grew up thinking we were full brother and sister but then, one time when Mum and Dad had split up (which happened quite a lot), Mum introduced us to this man she said was Ryan's "real dad". I think Ryan was about six at the time and he was really churned up about it. He adored our dad and told Mum he didn't want another one, but Mum said he had to get to know this stranger called Dave. Neither me nor Ryan liked Dave coz he had a nasty temper. We saw him hit Mum once, which our own dad would never do. Then Dave moved out and our real dad moved back in.

I think our dad – I suppose I ought to call him *my* dad – knew all along that Ryan wasn't his son but I don't think that mattered to him. He always treated him well coz he was a decent guy, a bit weak maybe to walk away and leave us all those times, and then to bugger off to America for ever, but I think Mum probably drove him to it. He did try and stay in touch with us, but I don't think Mum made it that easy for him. She told social services he'd been violent with her, although I'm 100 per cent sure she'd mixed him up with Dave, so they didn't exactly encourage him to have a lot to do with us.

Me and Ryan had been in and out of care a few times when Mum wasn't well but we always got a place together. But when social services realised that Mum was never going to be able to care for us at home, some trainee social worker decided that Ryan should be with his "own family" rather than staying with me, who'd been there for him since he was born. It wasn't like his dad actually wanted him, so he had to go and live with this mean old grandmother and an even more hideous aunt, coz they had this thing about "family sticking together", though I suspect it was all about them wanting the allowance they managed to get paid for having him. That was before those two old witches showed their true colours and beat the crap out of Ryan, which is when he got moved. He went to live with some other foster carers, who were OK but not the right people for him, and that's why he now lives with J and M. Which is best for him coz they're brilliant, and it means I've got my brother and my foster carers and my BF/foster sister all in one place.

Anyway, Ryan got this letter last year from this woman, Susanna, who he hadn't even known existed. Susanna had always suspected her dad might have other kids but she didn't know for sure until she had this row with Evil Granny who told her that all her *grandchildren* were "ungrateful brats". Susanna asked around a bit and found out that she had a younger brother, my brother Ryan, and she got in touch.

Ryan was dead curious about seeing his newly discovered sister but a bit scared too, so I went along with him, which is what he asked me to do. Jane drove us there and she went shopping while me and Susanna and Ryan drank lots of tea and coke and ate stale sandwiches in a supermarket café. It wasn't the kind of place I'd have chosen for a meeting but Susanna suggested it, and as me and Jane didn't know the town where she lives we went along with it. Ryan didn't seem to care much about the meeting place, he just wanted to know what his sister looked like. He's seen her a couple of times since then on his own, when she's come down here and they've met for a bit of tea. They ring each other sometimes but he doesn't tell me a lot about her. I think he guesses that I'm not that crazy about her.

I mean she's nice enough. She's kind and gentle and she loves animals and soap operas, and she reads all the celebrity magazines and watches all the TV shows on Saturday nights. But she doesn't seem to have much of a real "life". She told us that she works in a small company that makes parts for computers or something, and she's the secretary to the company director. She really loves her job, which is great, and she's got two friends there, but they sound like they're about twice her age, and both with husbands and grown-up kids of their own.

The thing with this Susanna is that she's not like us. I mean she's OK, but she's well... I mean she's sooooo boring. She's only 25 but she's going on 48. Really frumpy. She's one of those neat little people who buys clothes that will last a hundred years without ever wearing out, and flat sensible shoes. She's also one of those types who wears a little bit of pale blue eye shadow, just on their lids, like really old people do, without any eyeliner or mascara. And she wears pearly pink lipstick and pale pink acrylic cardigans. I picture her living in this neat little flat, where everything has a place and there's a calendar with kittens on the kitchen wall, and a picture of a sunset hanging over the radiator in the sitting room and a tapestry she embroidered herself saying something like, "Home is where the heart is", and some pink carnations in a jug on the table... Yeah I know, I'm being a bit of a cow to judge her like that, but I can't stand people who want to get old before they've been young. If they're like that in their 20s, what're they going to be like when they get to 40 or 50? It doesn't bear thinking about.

But there is one thing that me and Ryan and this Susanna have in common. We all hate their dad, Dave. Susanna's mum was a bit like our mum, coz she also had some mental health problems and she let him pick on her when she was dead vulnerable. In fact, I think it was worse for Susanna coz Dave stayed around for the early part of her childhood. We also all hate Mad Aunt and Evil Granny. It seems that pair of witches bullied Susanna's mum when she tried to walk out on Dave and wouldn't let her leave. So the poor woman stayed and got mega depressed and got taken into hospital – like our mum and also like us. Susanna got taken into care when she was about four or five, but then her mum's mum came and took her to live with her, and she grew up with her grandparents, which is maybe why she's such an "old" kind of person.

Anyway, Ryan seems determined to think that Susanna is snubbing him on purpose, or something. I don't know what that's about. Jane told me his teacher says he's dead moody in class at the moment. Like if anyone upsets him in any way he goes into a total meltdown, and he's ultra defensive if anyone criticises him. Jane thinks it's just a phase, coz he's had a tough year too.

He hated having to give evidence in the court case, even though they let him do it through this remote TV link, so he didn't actually have to be in the court room. It was like he blamed everyone for making him do it, which I thought was dead weird. I didn't see why he couldn't understand that we needed to do it for Nathan, but he said that nothing was going to bring Nathan back so what did it matter? I said it did matter because Nathan didn't deserve to die and the men had to be brought to justice, and Ryan said everyone dies, and I said that was crazy. But then sometimes he says that Nathe is lucky coz he doesn't have to 'live with all the crap' and I don't get why he feels like that. Sure, life is hard at times but you can't give up. You have to just keep on keeping on like Jane, coz you never know what's round the next corner. And sometimes when you look back like a month, or six months or even a year later, you think, 'Why did I feel like that?' or 'Why did I sweat so much about that thing?' because then you've got it all in perspective and it doesn't seem like a real problem any more.

But then Jane also says that some kids do get very depressed in adolescence and Ryan has also been a bit like that. He's much more like Mum than me. I got some of Mum's stubbornness, her way of believing that what she says is always right (yeah, I know I'm not a saint) and Ryan got more of her sensitive side, the self-destruct button bit of Mum that always sees the worst in everything and digs herself in deeper and deeper. When stuff goes wrong, I've got this strong survival thing that makes me want to come out fighting, but Ryan's always coped by running away and turning everything in on himself.

Yeah well – I can't sort my brother out tonight, so I got to sleep now, Diary. Shouldn't have drunk all that coffee today. I was never much of a coffee girl until I worked at that place and they got all those yummy flavours like hazelnut and mint choc and choccy orange...

Sean phoned tonight and we had an argument. Well, not an argument exactly but he knew I was pretty mad at him.

It all started OK with me telling him about my day at the college café and him telling me about his day at uni. I told him that Lucy still hadn't given me a definite answer about that party I want her to come to and he said, 'Just give her time,' adding, 'It would take me forever to get over it if you got murdered, Holly.'

'Yeah but we're not talking about "getting over it",' I corrected him. 'You don't "get over" something like that. You just learn to manage it.'

'Hark at you, Holly, you sound like a textbook or something,' Sean teased me. (He's probably right. You don't grow up with loads of social workers in your life without getting to know all their jargon.)

'The thing is,' I said, 'something doesn't seem quite "right" with Lucy. I know she's broken-hearted and still a bit in shock, but it's this wanting to be alone with Ruby all the time that worries me. Luce's always wanted to be around people. She hates being alone, or at least she used to, but now she doesn't even want to be with her mum and dad. She stays up there in the flat all by herself.'

'You worried that she's not looking after Ruby properly?' Sean asked and I felt slightly irritated with him. It was one thing for me to criticise Lucy but it wasn't something anyone else was allowed to do.

'She's a brilliant mother, really brilliant,' I informed him. 'She gives that child all her attention. She's always playing with her and doing stuff with her. It's just that they never seem to leave the flat, apart from when she takes Ruby to the toddlers group or the playground or for some check-up.'

'But doesn't Jane do anything? Or Martin? Aren't they worried about her?'

I explained to Sean that yes, J and M were a bit worried and this was all part of why they wanted me to be around when they went to Santa Land. 'But it's OK, I said, coz between the two of us we can get her out and doing stuff.'

There was silence on the other end of the phone for a while and then Sean said, 'When is that Santa trip thingy, Hols?'

I reminded him of the date and there was another pause. And then he said, 'Ah,' which didn't sound too good.

'Is there a problem?' I asked, already guessing the answer.

'Well, it's... you know how much I was looking forward to being with you Hols, don't you? ' Sean stopped and said very quickly, 'Look, it's Mum, it's my mum. She has to have an op in the new year and so Dad's agreed we can go to Australia for Christmas. All of us – me too. Mum is insisting.'

I didn't know what to say, so I didn't say anything.

'The thing is Hol... well, it's not exactly what I want either. It's a total pain coz the band had this little gig around Christmas, and I was kind of hoping we wouldn't be able to cancel it, but this new manager, Kate, says there will be other times and places and I should prioritise my family. Maybe the ticket sales weren't doing that well but ... I wish you'd never persuaded me to get a woman as manager Hols, they're far too understanding!'

But it was no good him trying to make light of this. I'd been so looking forward to us having our first proper Christmas together. Christmas can be a bit of a crappy time when you're in care and it brings back lots of memories and stuff, so I like to keep as busy as possible. We'd been invited to have Chrissle lunch with J and M and then, miracle of miracles, I'd actually been invited to Sean's family for Christmas evening, for a second dinner. Eating all that food was going to be a big challenge but that wasn't the point. I guess it was his father who'd pulled the strings on that one, coz me and Sean's mum will never see eye to eye. She's never going to think some girl from care is good enough for her son, but his dad and I are good mates and he'd argued that I was very much a part of Sean's life so I ought to be treated as part of the family.

And then there was Davina's masked ball thingy on New Year's Eve, and I'd already made Sean's costume.

I told him this.

'Oh Hols, don't you think I'd rather be there with you?'

'What? Instead of having a barbie on the beach in Australia, you mean?' I was shocked at how spiteful I sounded. It made me realise that I hadn't actually asked how bad this op was. So I did.

'Well, it's this cancer scare thing. You know she had the message to say they thought they'd found something and might need to do further tests. Well, they did find something and they don't really know how bad it is, so they need to explore further.'

Jane's friend Margaret had an exploratory op. It showed that if she hadn't had something done she might have got something nasty in 10 years' time. They just took out a little bit of something and she's been right as rain ever since. She told me all about it once at Martin's 50th birthday party, after she'd had too many glasses of wine.

Sean didn't seem reassured by Margaret's story. 'Yeah well, everyone is different, I guess. Mum doesn't know if it's serious or not at this stage. It might be nothing at all. Or it might be something to worry about, but the thing is Hols, she's dead scared.'

'And she's using that to make your dad change his mind about them going to Australia.' I know it was a horribly mean thing to say but I've just had it with that woman and the way she manipulates everyone and everything so she always gets her own way. Sean's poor dad had already said it really wasn't the best time for them to go visit her sister coz it had been a bit of a lousy year for business and they'd better wait a bit before seeing the new grand-niece or nephew or whatever it was.

'Yes… no. Honestly, Hols, Mum is freaking out a bit and Dad decided that going to Australia was probably the best way to calm her down, take her mind off it.'

'Couldn't they just have gone away for a couple of days, to a nice hotel or something… just the two of them? I don't see why you have to go, too,' I said, hoping he couldn't tell that I was holding back on the tears.

'Mum wants us all to be together. She's just so scared Hols. Her best friend from primary school died of cancer when she was only 32. She left two young kids…'

'Yeah, but that doesn't mean your mum's going to.'

'And it doesn't mean she's not. Look, I know you don't like my mum, but give her a break this time, Hols. She isn't all bad you know.'

'If you say so,' I said. OK, I wasn't exactly proud of myself, but honestly, that woman gets her own way all the time. No matter what it takes. I seriously wonder if she really is that worried or whether she's milking the situation.

Sean sighed big time. 'Look, I think we need to agree to differ on this. I don't want us to fall out. Tell me what's going down at the garden centre.'

So I told him that today I'd painted and sold five gnomes. Rhonda has set up this great system where people pay their deposit and leave a photo and any instructions about how they want the gnome to look. I then paint it when I'm next in and the customer comes and picks it up when it's ready. Sean said it was brilliant and we chatted a bit more about this and that. But I was still dead upset about Australia.

Sean said, 'Love you, Hols,' before he ended the call and I just mumbled 'You too.' I can't stop thinking that if he really did love me he'd have refused to go with them. But I need to stop thinking about that now. I need a decent night's sleep. I'm going to have a lie-in tomorrow. My first in ages and I've earned it.

SATURDAY 3 DECEMBER

I was woken up by a phone call from Jane. If it was anyone else I'd have probably told them where to stuff it, but I knew Jane wouldn't call unless it was something important.

What she wanted to know was whether I'd had any contact with Ryan since supper on Monday. I said he'd told me about Susanna cancelling.

'Yes, he seems very upset about that,' Jane told me. 'Extremely upset in fact, because he's refused to come out of his room since he got her message.'

'What, not at all? Not to use the bathroom or eat or anything?'

'Fortunately he is "using the bathroom" so we haven't had to give him a bucket. Yet. But he waits till we're downstairs and he just goes in and out. If we do see him on the landing he just brushes straight past us and goes back into the bedroom.'

'But I mean, can't you stop him going in?'

'Well, we could. Martin and I have both tried standing in front of his bedroom door to try and get him to talk to us, but he just hunkers down on the landing and curls up like a hibernating animal and goes back to sleep. To be honest, we're a bit surprised he's so upset about Susanna. He always moans about her being so boring, says she's nothing like you, Holly. He really cares about you, you know, though I suspect he never tells you.

'Anyway, he just gazes into space. I called the mental health services people and a community psychiatric nurse came out yesterday but he couldn't get a word out of him either. He said he didn't think there was too much to worry about and Ryan was just trying to make some kind of point. So he's still there. Lying on his bed and looking at the ceiling and then walking to the lavatory every now and again. I think he may even be washing a bit and cleaning his teeth – he doesn't seem to smell – but not a single word.'

'Is he eating at all?' I asked, knowing what a dustbin my brother can be.

'Yes, yes, he's eating now because I'm putting a tray outside his door. For a day, I refused to do that in the hope he'd get hungry and come down, but then I realised the silly boy was probably going to starve himself.' Jane gave a heavy sigh.

'And he hasn't fallen out with any of his mates?'

'No. Well, not as far as we can tell. He was chatting away happily to some mates on the phone the night before. The twins have been round today, asking for him, and he wouldn't see them, but he doesn't seem to have had a row with them or anything. I had to make up some excuse about him feeling awful with flu, which is what I've told the school as well because I don't want them making a lot of fuss. That would be worse for him.'

'And what about... Well, he hasn't gone and fallen for some boy who's rejected him?' I asked, though I was pretty sure Ryan's heart still belonged to the Corries' star player, Rashan Gayle. He's a bit of a perfectionist and I can't see him falling for any mere mortal.

'No sign of that, Hols, but I guess I'd be the last person to know if he had. I get the feeling this is something to do with Susanna postponing their meeting. He seemed so angry with her for doing it. You don't think he was hoping she'd ask him to stay for Christmas do you? We wouldn't have minded if he'd wanted to go to hers.'

'I doubt it,' I told her, equally mystified. 'I mean he likes that he's got this other sister but I think he'd die of boredom spending more than a couple of hours with her. And he's got lots of plans with his mates for over Christmas. He was dead chuffed the twins' mum has asked him there for Boxing Day.'

Jane gave an even bigger sigh. 'To be honest Hols, I feel such a failure. Never in all my years as a foster carer have I handled anything so badly. I'm usually good at getting young people to talk but...'

Poor Jane. She works so hard and always tries her best to do the right thing. She can also be tough as old boots when a kid seriously pushes the boundaries and there's a risk that they're going to hurt someone. She's talked kids off window ledges, soothed teenagers into handing over knives, stayed calm during 24-hour temper tantrums where every window in the house got smashed and a few bombs got detonated on the front lawn. (OK, maybe I'm exaggerating just slightly...) Now my beastly little brother with his sulking silence had defeated her. I'd kill him when I got my hands on him.

'Of course, he's not had the easiest couple of years but he'd seemed better after the court case was over. Then this moodiness, these patches of seeming so angry with the whole world started getting worse, just as I thought he was starting to settle down and feeling more secure with us,' Jane told me sadly.

I'd thought so too. Ryan has been through a lot but he's also had some really good times. He'd been recognised as a hero by the local community, made some great new mates and he'd been made captain of the football team, which had been his ultimate dream.

'And he does seem keen on the Lapland trip, if you count not wanting to be left out, keen. To be honest, though, I was surprised. I thought he'd consider it far too babyish.'

I told Jane that I'd been a bit mystified by my brother's response but had assumed it was because he wanted to capture something of the "perfect Christmas" that children who've never had a proper family Christmas dream about.

'Yes, I do wonder if it's the Christmas thing that is getting to Ryan. I know it can be an emotional time.'

Yes, it can, but I also knew that my brother was pretty thrilled about the iPad he knew that J and M had organised for his Christmas present. Boys of his age are so materialistic, and I'd had the strong impression that at 16 that mattered a whole lot more than the happy family stuff. But you can't tell, especially with boys. And my brother can be dead weird when he puts his mind to it.

'D'you want me to come over? Talk to him?' I asked.

'I wasn't going to ask you to do that,' Jane explained. 'I know you're really busy at work at the moment. It was more that I hoped you might have some ideas. You know Ryan better than any of us.'

I love that about Jane – the way she treats me like I'm the one who knows my brother best. I said I could go over in the evening, after work, but Jane said not to worry. It was important for me and Lucy to have our girls' night out together – for both our sakes.

Anyway now I need to stop writing you, Diary, and get my act together. I'm meeting my foster sister in an hour at the bus stop. I hope she:

A. Turns up

B. Doesn't fret about Ruby all evening

C. Doesn't decide to go home 20 mins after she arrives

D. Doesn't drive me crazy so's we have a big bust-up.

Actually I can take care of D myself by making sure I don't let her wind me up. A to C are kind of up to her but I can also make sure she has a good time so she doesn't want to go home. And I can do that by letting her talk about whatever it is she needs to talk about. This isn't about me. This evening is about her, and getting her to stop living like some hermit crab. I need to remember that.

SUNDAY 4 DECEMBER

I did the morning shift at the café which was pretty quiet. Just a few students in using the library and some locals who know we do the cheapest cappuccino in the area. Everyone sits bleary-eyed over the Sunday papers, pretending they're reading about world affairs but half of them are just looking at the photos and catching up on which singer flashed her knickers while getting out of a taxi and which footballer scored an own goal by snoggin' his missus' best friend... and then I came back here and had a longish snooze. This evening I've been doing a bit of sewing.

Me and Lucy had a good time last night. Well, at least I think we did. There's something I can't put my finger on, so maybe writing it here will help me work out why I have this kind of niggly feeling that something still wasn't quite right.

To start with, Luce just wanted to talk about Ruby, which is kind of normal. She was a bit hyper and she had this definite smell of alcohol on her breath that I guessed she'd had for Dutch courage. She said that she'd made J and M promise that if Ruby wouldn't settle they'd ring her immediately and she might have to go home. I said that was fine with me, because I knew that Ruby would settle with her granny and granddad.

Then Luce wanted to talk about Nathan, which was also OK with me. I remember Nathe as a kind of second kid brother with me as his bossy flatmate. We lived together at St Mark's Crescent, the independent living place where I first met him and Keesh. He wasn't much younger than me but he seemed dead young somehow – sweet and immature and not at all sophisticated like his sister. He and Keesh couldn't live together in the same flat as they drove each other insane, but I was good for him coz I wasn't really his sister and he was more scared of making me mad. He could be a slob at times, but I guess that's true of a lot of people, girls as well as boys. I used to nag him and give him quite a hard time.

But Lucy remembers him differently. He was the boy she loved, who loved her and loved the baby she'd had by another bloke. She has warm, soft, fluffy memories of Nathe, who did everything he could to please her. So I tried not to feel awkward when she talked about how much she missed the silky feel of his skin, the soft, tight wool of his hair as he slept with his head on her shoulder, his sweet kissable lips and the way he looked her in the eye when... While all the time I wanted to say, 'Shut up, Lucy, this makes me feel queasy!' It was a bit like someone telling me romantic stuff about Ryan, and you don't really want to think about your brother in *that* way.

Anyway, Lucy had made an effort with her appearance and I was dead impressed. I could see a couple of lads checking her out on the bus and Lucy saw them doing it. She was fussing with the hemline of her sparkly little pink dress, which was just a bit short but showed off her smooth legs magnificently. Luce will never be a size 10, or even 12, but she is utterly gorgeous and men are always drooling over her. Makes me wish sometimes I wasn't so long and skinny and had more curves like hers. She'd pulled her blonde hair into a loose bun and curls were escaping down her neck, and she'd done her make-up really well, so that her eyelids were all shimmery like the dress. She'd also put on glittery lip gloss and she smelt just wonderful, like jasmine on a summer's evening. Our Lucy was quite the party animal. I hoped that the party I was taking her to would be worthy of her efforts.

Actually, it was a pretty good party. Dan was there with Rani, who was back from uni for her sister's engagement or something, and it seemed they were all loved up and happy. Even though I'd never say it to Dan, I did wonder if she'd dump him for a doctor or dentist or vet or someone posh with the kind of career prospects her parents have got their beady eyes on, but she does seem to be really into him.

Dan is good mates with the guys who were holding the party and Rani had brought two of her girl cousins with her. A few other girls had come along but there were still more boys than girls, so Lucy got loads of attention, just like I'd promised her. The thing about Lucy is that whether she means to be or not, she's a natural flirt. She's just one of those girls who knows how to look at a bloke, who knows just when to flick her hair or put her hand on his arm. She also knows how to pout her super-sexy lips and you just have to laugh as you watch the poor bloke going all hot and dizzy. I asked her once if she knew she was doing it and she turned all huffy on me and asked if I was calling her a slag. I said I'd never call anyone a slag coz that's what boys call girls when they behave in ways that boys think only they should be allowed to behave in.

Anyway, Lucy was born to flirt like birds were born to fly, and I realised that the problem was that she'd been shut away in her nest for far too long. Put her in a party situation and she just couldn't help herself. Soon she had this little gaggle of lads round her, all hanging on her every word and wanting her to dance. But she wouldn't dance with any of them; she just came and danced with me and Dan and Rani. Some of the guys kind of tried to muscle in a bit, but Lucy just manoeuvred herself so she was always facing me. She knew they were there and looked more alive than I'd seen her for a very long time.

We didn't stay very late but Rani had her sister's car and gave us a lift back to my place, which was really nice of her. I asked her and Dan to come in for coffee and the four of us sat round for a bit talking about this and that. Lucy did text Jane a bit to check that Ruby was doing OK, but she didn't seem to be in a big hurry for her dad to come and fetch her. She said she'd probably have another nip of Baileys to prepare her for the cold and I said that it looked more like half a pint she'd poured, and she just laughed. (I hope Keesh won't be too mad coz her ex-boyf bought her that and we were kind of saving it for New Year.)

I walked out to the car with Lucy so I could say hi to Martin. He looked so pleased when he saw that Lucy was all pink-cheeked and smiley. He would have hung around a bit for a chat, but Lucy started looking at her watch and he got the hint.

'We must do this again,' I said as I hugged her goodbye.

'Yeah, it was fun,' she answered, but there was something in her voice that made me wonder if she would come out again. It worried me a bit. Nobody should be totally sensible all the time, especially at 18. Even Jane goes out "with the girls" sometimes, although I think they just go round to her friends' houses and watch weepy movies and drink wine. But what do I know? They might hit the clubs sometimes and give us young ones a run for our money. Hmmm. Not sure I want to think about Jane freakin' out on the dance floor with all her flabby bits wobbling!

Rani and Dan didn't hang around much after Lucy left but Rani said that she thought Lucy was "very pretty". I don't think Rani has met many girls like Lucy. I used to have a bit of a downer on Rani because I thought she was a bit of a princess but I like her more now I know she got a hard time from her parents because she wasn't as clever as her sibs. Her parents didn't approve of her doing art when they wanted her to be a doctor or dentist like her sisters, but they had to eventually accept she wasn't as good at passing exams as the others, coz she has dyslexia and it wasn't recognised till she was quite old. It's made her even more determined to prove she can be brilliant at something creative. She's not bad at all really, maybe not quite as good as some of the other people who were in our year (if I'm honest, I don't think she's anywhere like as good as me) but she's got determination and she deserved to get into uni.

MONDAY 5 DECEMBER

Just a normal day at the college caf. Nothing exciting 'cept Dan came to say hello and we had a delivery of some yummy new lemon donuts.

But this evening when Keesh got in I had this feeling I could hear her crying. When I went and tapped on her door, she was all mascara-streaked round the eyes although she said she was fine. I made her some hot chocolate and she had a little cry, and she told me how she'd been thinking about Nathe all day and how she was never going to see him again. I told her that Lucy had been talking about Nathe, too, and then I cried a bit and me and Keesh had a big hug and we added a bit of Baileys to the hot chocolate. We then sat up for like another two hours and started remembering all those silly things Nathe used to do and say, and what fun we had those months when all of us lived in the same house. And how Lucy and Nathe used to pretend that they weren't crazy about each other, but every time we turned our backs they'd be kissing or holding hands and behaving like love-struck idiots in Romeo and Juliet or something ('cept it was the modern version where Juliet already has a bump coz of some lad from the rival gang).

TUESDAY 6 DECEMBER

I was late getting up this morning and not in a very good mood, but I'd promised Jane I'd go round and see my delightful little brother, only to find he'd actually got up and gone to school. Jane was as surprised as I was coz she'd thought he was still sulking in his room and going nowhere. 'But then he appeared in the kitchen, demanding his football kit,' Jane told me. 'And you could have knocked me over with a feather, but I said nothing and just found it for him. He asked me for his bus fare and off he went, like he'd been going to school every day. I told him to tell people he'd had flu. I shouldn't really encourage him to lie, but what can you do?'

I'm sure my brother will make up some story about having a tropical illness or being involved in some incredibly complicated accident. He'd never tell them he's been feeling depressed, but then he'd never admit to getting just a plain old cold or sickness bug either. He'll always come up with some kind of elaborate story. The other kids will know he's lying and he'll know they know, but being the hero who chased the guys that murdered Nathan has given my brother this kind of kudos at school, and people seem to like his wild stories. He'll make a really good actor or a writer or something, one day. Maybe he'll become that performance poet me and Martin were talking about ☺.

It's always nice to see Jane and we had a quick coffee together and I told her a bit of my recent news. I hoped Lucy might come down and join us so I texted her, but she said she had period pains and was staying in bed. I said I'd ring her later, which I did, on my way to my late shift at the garden centre.

Lucy sounded a bit bleary although it was nearly one o'clock. It's OK for some people who can laze about in bed all day and don't have jobs or college to go to. But I suppose she has to get up with Ruby in the night and early this morning, coz little kids have their own body clocks.

I asked Lucy if she'd had a good time at the party the other night and she asked me if I remembered this boy called Aiden coz he'd been texting her a lot. I said I remembered a lot of boys but I hadn't really paid any of them a lot of attention. 'Was he one of those guys that was round us when we were dancing?' I asked and she laughed. 'No, he was a bit too cool for that.'

I asked her to describe him and she said he was blonde and fit, which told me nothing much at all. I asked her if she was going to see him again, and she retorted, 'Of course not, he was a jerk... and I don't want a boyfriend.'

Then she said that she thought that Rani and Dan were a cute couple, and she liked the way they have this secret smile they give each other when they think nobody is looking... And then she went on about this Aiden bloke a bit more and how he'd chased her with this bit of mistletoe when she went to the kitchen. While she was telling me Lucy got all giggly and silly, and started to hiccup coz she wasn't breathing properly.

OMG – what is it with everyone at the moment? Is it coz it's nearly Christmas and there are all those cheesy songs playing everywhere you go? I just wish everyone would get a grip. This includes my boyf who texted this evening to ask if I'd got the flowers he sent me as a kind of apology for letting me down over the Australia thing. I rang him and said thank you for the flowers, but I hadn't seen any and he didn't have to send them anyway. He then got all cross with the flower delivery company and I told him that the old bat downstairs had probably taken them in and kept them for herself because she hates me and Keesh. She hates us both because we're young but she hates Keesh even more because she's black, and she mumbles stuff about us under her breath if ever we pass her on the stairs. Keesh cornered her once and said, 'Lady, if you have a problem you better come right out and say it, coz I'm sick of you mumblin' and cussin' and pullin' faces every time I sees you,' and the woman kind of looked frightened coz I guess she's a coward underneath all that mumbling, and she went scuttling into her front door like the cockroach she reminds me of.

Sean said I should go down and ask her, but I said what's the point? She'll only lie about it, and she'll have thrown them away or hidden them or something and there was nothing I could do. Sean said he thought I could at least ask her. I wanted to say that I had better things to do with my time than knock on the door of toothless old biddies whose flats smell of frying food and rotting rubbish, but then I thought maybe that sounded ungrateful about the flowers, so we agreed that he'd check with the delivery company and see if they could tell him anything. If they said they'd left them with the woman downstairs, I'd go in guns blazing (not literally of course, but sometimes I think it might be a good idea).

Sean says the flowers are white and red roses, which is kind of dead romantic. And I know they'd have cost him a lot and he's saving to go to Australia and he never has much money anyway. But I'm not the sentimental type so I shan't be upset if they don't get delivered. It's the thought that counts, isn't it?

Something totally freaky happened today. I was painting a set of comedy braces on a gnome when I heard this person say, 'Excuse me, young woman,' and I looked up to see this dead glamorous middle-aged woman, who was trying to get my attention. She was one of those women who look like they just walked out of some fashion advert, in a pair of designer jeans and a little jacket and some really cool leather boots. But there was also something a little bit familiar about her shiny bobbed brown hair, the way she held her head and those deep green eyes.

'Can I help you?' I asked, putting on an instant smile and feeling very scruffy in my paint-splattered overalls.

'I most certainly hope so,' she said, with this hint of a really cool French accent. She had one of those voices that sounds like she definitely means business, coz she's used to being in control. 'Can you tell me where I can find an amaryllis?'

I was giving her directions when someone walked up behind her – except it wasn't just "someone"! It was this face I'd last seen about two-and-a-half years ago, on one of the days of my life I'd really rather forget. And seeing it again made my chest go all tight with this complete mix of panic and anger.

My anger must have been strongest, coz he took one look at my face and stopped in his tracks, like a rabbit caught in the headlights. But his frozen state didn't last for long and he smiled, and his amazing green eyes shone and for one moment my stupid, crazy heart did the tiniest somersault. Until I told it off and got it back in check, and I made sure I had the sternest look possible on my face.

The woman was asking me another question but I couldn't concentrate, and he must have seen that, coz he said, 'C'mon Mum, let's get that wretched plant bought. We still need to pick up the compost that Dad asked for.'

So she was his mum. It was dead obvious really. She looked so totally like the determined and mega-successful news reporter he'd told me about – the woman who took photos of children and lost tribes, who risked her neck on battlefields and blagged her way into terrorist camps. And she definitely had that icy-cold edge he'd often moaned about. You couldn't see any kid wanting to climb on her knee for a cuddle or a goodnight kiss.

Hey, what was I thinking about? I wasn't interested in one tiny little detail of this guy's life. None of it was any excuse for the stupid, dangerous stuff he'd done. Yet there he was, turning back to look at me as he led his mother away, mouthing something to me that looked a bit like 'Catch you later'. I couldn't believe the freaking nerve of him! Did he really think I was going to get into some kind of top-secret stuff with him, the idiot who'd turned my life upside down?

I refused to catch his eye as I watched the two of them heading out of sight towards the winter shrubs section. It was down an aisle and round a corner, so with any luck I wouldn't have to see him again. My hands were shaking like crazy as I tried to paint the outline of the stripy braces on "Johnny the Office Joker". I'd just managed to finish it when the punter who'd ordered it returned.

'You've really got his stupid grin and his gappy teeth,' the customer exclaimed, handing over the second half of his money (we make them pay a deposit before I start any of the work). 'And I like what you've done with his braces, the way they're kind of wiggly like they're too loose and his trousers are about to fall off.'

He was wittering on and I wasn't really listening, coz my mind was whirring like a hamster on a wheel.

I just wished that Nessa was already back from uni. I love it when she's working in the garden centre coz she's just the best person ever to have around. She's kind and quiet, and gentle and sensible but she's also good at noticing stuff and asking these questions that really make you think. I wouldn't be surprised if she trained to be a therapist or something when she's got the old ruins stuff out of her head ☺.

Because Ness wasn't there, I started imagining what she'd say to me and how I'd answer her:

Ness: So who is this boy, Holly? And what's his hold over you?

Me: He hasn't got a "hold" over me, Ness. He's just a guy I dated a while back and now he's history.

Ness: So what's the problem then? You seem very upset.

Me: Nothing really – except he nearly killed my little brother with a heroin overdose.

Ness: Ah, that would explain everything.

Me: Yes, it would.

Ness: But what I still don't quite understand, Holly, is why your heart still does that little somersault every time you see him.

Me: How do you know it does that?

Ness: Because I'm sitting inside your head. I can hear and see a lot of things.

Me: Oh yeah, I guess you can.

Ness: So what is it then? Can you tell me?

Me: You mean you haven't noticed the colour of his eyes?

Ness: Well, sure. They are rather striking...

Me: Well, it's just the eyes. That's what I fell for when I first saw him, and he's the guy I first... well, you know, I mean he was the first...

Ness: Ah, I see.

Me: No, you don't. There's nothing to "see". It's not like that any more. I hate him Ness, I really hate that guy.

Ness: So you say.

Me: You don't sound like you believe me.

Ness: It's not me you have to convince.

I was about to explain to Ness why I thought I had got Ptolemy completely out of my head, when I realised he was standing in front of me, waiting for me to notice him. Had my lips been moving while I had my little "chat" with Ness? I hoped not, although really, why should I care?

'Yes?' I snapped, though maybe I should've ignored him. 'Did you want something?'

'Yes... no... I mean,' he was almost stuttering in his effort to get the words out. 'Look Holly. I just wanted to say... Well, I wanted to say that I was sorry. Really, really sorry. I know sorry isn't enough but...'

'Yeah, you're right. Sorry isn't enough,' I spat the words back at him. 'He could've died!'

'I know. I realised that. It was like... well, it was like a wake-up call for me. I went to ground for a bit, went over to my mum's family in France, and I'm clean these days, Holly.'

'Well bully for you! It was nearly a "death call" for my poor brother,' I replied, amazed that I hadn't started screaming and yelling and calling this jerk every swear word under the sun. 'And you know what? I really don't care if you're clean or not. It's of no interest to me whatsoever.'

It was good saying those words; it got a lot off my chest. It also felt a bit unreal, like I was a heroine in some old-fashioned movie, telling the hero he was a "cad and a bounder".

I moved away and started putting the lids on the paint pots.

'I know. Look, I totally understand why you probably hate me but if you ever want to talk about it... or if there's anything I can ever do for you, just some way to show how sorry I am...' He was talking to my back now, but that was his tough luck.

'So I don't call the cops and tell them I've seen you?' I hissed at him from between my teeth.

I'd often lain awake at night and thought about the things I would say to this weasel if he ever came near me again, and how nice it would be to call up the central police station and say, 'I want to report the address of a guy who nearly killed a teenage boy by letting him overdose on heroin.' But somehow this meeting didn't feel quite as good as I'd hoped. Maybe because so much other crap had happened in the meantime – like Nathan's murder.

'I know. I understand,' was how Tol replied to that. 'Yeah, I know it's what I deserve, so you must do that if you need to, Hols.'

At that moment I knew I wouldn't because I realised he'd probably been worrying about it every day since it happened, wondering if he'd get picked up for what he'd done. It seemed a pretty good kind of punishment, but I just said, 'Yes, that's what you deserve.'

'Anyway, Holly,' he said, slipping a piece of paper onto the workbench beside me. 'You must do what you think is best. This is my telephone number... for the police or for you to call me if you ever want to talk.'

And then he was gone. And it took me five minutes to get my breathing calm enough to finish the clearing up.

Ness: Are you going to throw that piece of paper away?

(OMG, I'd completely forgotten that Ness was still in my head watching this happen!)

Me: Probably not. Coz I might need it if I decide to contact the police.

Ness: I see.

Me: No Ness – there's nothing to "see". I told you that before.

Ness: It's OK Holly, I believe you. Now we'd better get this mess cleared up before Marje spots it.

If only Ness was really there to help with the clearing up. I'd somehow knocked two paint tin lids onto the floor and a large patch of blue paint and a small patch of red were drying into the concrete. Fortunately Duane happened to be passing with a broom and doing his usual sneaking a peak at me and blushing routine. I decided to put him to work and sent him off to find some turpentine and greasy rags from the chemicals store. He'd have to get Rhonda to unlock it and that would take ages. By which time, I'd have moved the rest of my stuff and be out of the way of those pathetic baby animal squashed by a car eyes he makes at me. Now if his eyes were a beautiful green I might be just a tiny bit interested, if I didn't already have Sean of course ☺.

I was carrying the pots back to the store when Marje stopped me. 'You look very pale, pet,' she said, 'and your hands are shaking. That's not like you.' I looked down and saw that the paint pot in my right hand was doing a kind of jig, so I let Marje steer me towards a chair. She even went and got me some water. Marje is an alright sort really. We've had our moments in the past but she now realises that I'm one of her best workers, and she trusts me.

'You look like you've seen a ghost,' she told me, not very helpfully, as she handed over the water.

Yeah, well I suppose I had, but I shook my head. 'Think maybe I was concentrating too hard, doing the braces on the gnomes can be quite tricky...'

'And they're lovely pet, they're going down very well but they do seem to take you rather a long time. There was something I wanted to say...'

'Well that's very kind,' I said, seizing my moment. 'And yes, there is the extra cost from the paint I've had to bring in and my brushes and stuff, and it would be nice if you could pay me a little something for the extra work. Maybe 25 per cent would be fair.'

'Er well, that wasn't exactly...'

But Marje didn't get a chance to say any more because I decided that it was a perfect moment to give into this feeling of dizziness that had started to come over me. 'Can you pass me that water again?' I asked and took a big slug.

When I'd finished the glass, I stood up. 'Thanks so much, Marje,' I said. 'I feel much better now. And the little bonus will help. Shall I tell Rhonda to add it to my pay packet on Saturday?' I grabbed my paint pots and walked off quickly before she could say anything. My hands were still shaking a little bit as I got to the storeroom, but overall I felt a lot stronger again.

Sean phoned this evening and I wondered if I should say something about Ptolemy, but I'd never really come clean with Sean about the guy who had half-killed my little brother. He just knew it was some bloke that was hanging around when him and me split up. I hadn't made it clear that he was someone I was "seeing". Anyway I was still pretty upset with him about the Christmas thing.

So we talked about some film he'd seen about someone who did something to someone who did something to someone else, but I'm not quite sure what, and then someone got shot, which is pretty standard in those kind of films. Apparently it was all very tense and the special effects weren't as good as the previous film by the same director. But I can't remember anything about it at all because while he was telling me, I started thinking again about Tol appearing like that, out of the blue, and I couldn't really concentrate.

Sean did say that he'd rung the flower delivery company and they thought that maybe their courier had delivered the flowers to the wrong number. Sean had given them a hard time and said they had to deliver them again, which apparently they're going to do. I said that was really nice coz it's not every day that I get flowers, but Sean seemed a bit offended by that, like I was saying it was something he should be doing more often. We had this rather strained conversation about work, and I didn't tell him about the mini drama with Ryan, as it didn't seem that important.

Sometimes I wonder if relationships are just too much like hard work! Which reminds me about the message I got from Lucy earlier. Apparently she did text that guy she met at the party and he's asked her out. She tells me she's not going but that doesn't make a lot of sense coz she obviously likes him enough to chat with him by text. Or maybe she is just really lonely up there in her nest. I don't know and just now I don't care. I've got enough of my own stuff to concentrate on. If I don't get that jacket finished for Davina she certainly won't be paying me for it...

THURSDAY 8 DECEMBER

I spent the morning finishing off the jacket and dropped it off at the boutique on the way to afternoon lectures. Davina wasn't in when I first got there and Keesh told me she was out having coffee with her accountant, but she thought she'd be back soonish. Keesh looked pretty busy. One of their regular customers was in – seemed her husband had given her a great big fat cheque to buy herself a Christmas wardrobe, but she didn't seem that fussed. Maybe she's got so much money she's bored by all that shopping. I'd be sooooooo thrilled if someone did that for me, and I know exactly what I'd have from the shop. There's this little black cocktail dress with this old-fashioned bustle thing. It's so beautifully cut and would make me look like one of those totally elegant 1950s film stars, and there's this deep purple jacket with a fake fur collar that has my name written all over it. If only I had about 700 pounds to spend.

I sat on a chair in the corner and watched as Keesh laid out dresses and coats and trousers for the customer to look at. The woman would shake her head and say that nothing really appealed to her. Then, just as Keesh had put them back on the hanger, she'd say could she see that red dress again, and maybe the green silk trousers, but then she couldn't decide whether or not to try them on and she'd see a bag and want to know if Keesh had that in another colour. And while Keesh was looking in the stockroom she'd see a silk scarf and try that on, and then Keesh would come out with the bag in scarlet and she'd have decided that she didn't really want scarlet after all as she already has so many bags in that colour, but please could Keesh see if she had this scarf but with an orange border instead of the green one.

I had to take my hat off to Keesh. She was so patient. She knew just how to handle that woman. She never complained and she wasn't pushy, urging the woman to try things on or telling her that everything made her look amazing. But when she finally did take a few items into the changing room Keesh was very honest – nodding her head in approval when the woman came out in something that really flattered her and holding back her comments if she wasn't quite so sure. The woman started to ask Keesh for her opinion and soon Keesh was fetching a couple of other things from the rails – something in a slightly quieter or richer colour than the really bright colours she'd originally gone for. Before long the woman had a fitting room full of dresses, suits, skirts, trousers, shirts, tunics, coats and jackets – so many items that they were spilling out into the shop and Keesh had to fetch some extra chairs and hangers to stop them getting underfoot. And then there were all the accessories – the scarves, handbags, tights, shawls and shrugs that Keesha suggested would "finish" the outfit just perfectly.

'Well that was amazing,' I said, when the woman finally left with four bulging carrier bags. 'You are the most incredible saleswoman Keesh. No wonder Davina gave you a pay rise.'

'Well thank you kindly, girlfriend,' Keesh said, taking a mock bow, 'But you know what da real secret is?'

I shook my head. 'I guess there's not really a secret. Apart from you being a natural.'

Keesh acknowledged my comment with a modest little shrug of her shoulders. 'Well there is dat, but you know what? That lady is colourblind and she doesn't have no confidence in her own sense of style. So when she goes to other stores and they say, "Madam, you look wonderful in dat", even when it clashes so bad with her hair, and she buys it and takes it home. Then her hubby or her friends they say, "Babes, dat isn't yo' colour!" So she doesn't go back to those shops, but she come here coz she know we won't try to sell her stuff that doesn't look good on her. We let her look on her own for a bit and then ever so gently we start to make a few likkle suggestions.'

'Well, it works,' I said, 'It's great. I am totally impressed. But I wish you hadn't sold her my little black dress. I wanted that sooooooo badly.'

'Yeah well, she got the credit card to pay for it and you hasn't. Yo has to face facts, hun.'

Well that was true, but it still didn't seem fair.

'Hey stop sulkin', girl,' Keesh flicked my ponytail affectionately. 'She ain't never goin' to look as classy as you would in dat dress coz she hasn't got your legs. You could look good in a sack, girl, and she needs clothes dat are real expensive coz she won't ever look good in a sack.'

I love Keesh, she always knows how to make me feel good. I wish I could do the same for her. She's seemed a bit low recently. I don't blame her not wanting a man around who wasn't able to support her like she needed, but it's also quite hard to deal with a break-up not long after you've had a big loss. Lots of girls might have hung on in there, just to avoid that, but Keesh is so strong. She says when you're feeling sad it's better to only have people around you who really care about you, and she doesn't need a man just for the sake of having a boyf. She'd just have felt even more let down when he let her down, which he kept doing. She didn't blame him coz she knew he didn't really understand. He's one of those people who's lived his life in a cosy little bubble and he's never had to face up to someone dying or moving away or being on the other side of the world, which is what Keesh has had to cope with.

It's what most of us care leavers have had to face up to at some time or another. I don't know if it makes us better at dealing with sad stuff, but it makes us more aware of how these things affect people. So we give one another a bit more tolerance, a little bit more understanding, coz you know what it's like to be bruised really badly inside. And some wounds just never heal up completely, so when something new comes along and hurts you, you have to look after those old wounds as well.

'You are a genius – and a darling,' I said, giving Keesh a smacking great kiss on the cheek. 'Now where is that wretched Davina woman? I really want her to see this jacket. Otherwise I'll be fretting all day that she doesn't like it.'

'Chill, babes,' Keesh says, taking the bag I'd brought the jacket in out of my hands. 'You know she loves everything you do. She just Miss Extra Picky and she always wants it perfick. Hey girl, dis is really beautiful, even better than the sketches on paper.' She held the jacket up to the light and ran the silky fabric through her fingers. 'You a genius too, girl!'

Me and Keesh need to set up 'The Keesh and Holly Are Fab Club'. We shan't let anyone else join, which will be OK coz two is a great number for members.

Keesh persuaded me to leave the jacket with her and assured me she'd show it to Davina as soon as she got back. 'Not dat she's hardly gonna miss seein' it there, babes.' Keesh had hung it on the back of the changing room door, where it worked wonderfully against the dove grey paint I'd chosen to revamp the area. Davina loves her repaints and I love that she chooses me to do the styling for her – and employs me and Sean and Keesh to do the actual decorating. She gets us fabulous picnics when we're painting and she pays us really well. It's well worth giving up a free Sunday to paint for Davina. Makes up for the fact she can also be a really moody moo some days.

I hoped today wasn't going to be one of those days coz I really needed her to love the new jacket. She used to get a dressmaker to run up my designs but now she knows me better she trusts me to finish everything properly – and I've got dead good with the sewing machine. Attention to detail is what I'm really good at, and Davina recognises that.

I got the bus to college and did the afternoon shift. Kerry is back from her flu thing but she looked half dead on her feet. She says she daren't take any more time off coz she worries she might lose her job and she's got a four-year-old daughter to support. I said that surely nobody could be sacked for taking time off sick and there were laws to stop that happening. Anyway, she's the manager so she's in charge of the place. But she said that you could never be sure coz companies can restructure or decide to close a branch or something, so it's always good to show you're as willing as possible.

Oh and I had a conversation with my brother on the way into work. I hadn't spoken to him since the Bedroom Barricade, though I'd sent him a few texts and he'd even replied to one or two. I hadn't asked him anything about the weird stuff coz Ryan only talks about things when he's ready.

'Yeah, what do you want?' he asked, with all the usual charm of my brattish little brother.

'Oh sorry, did I disturb your breathing?' I replied with all the sarcasm of an irritated big sister. 'I forget that you need to concentrate when you do that.'

'Nah, I don't breathe,' Ryan replied. 'Breathing is so last year...'

'Fair enough,' I answered. 'Probably makes your life a lot easier. Are you still managing to talk, walk, sit and stand? I won't ask about thinking coz I know you've never been any good at that...'

'Big Sister, you kill me,' Ryan's tone dripped with so much sarcasm you could bottle it. 'You must have burnt up at least three brain cells thinking of that. Pity coz it means you've probably only got one left.'

'Two left,' I corrected, 'but my two brain cells are still a lot livelier than your six will ever be. So before those six pack up I need to ask you something.'

'Fire away,' Ryan replied. 'But better make it quick. I'm meant to be doing detention in the library but I slipped out for a cig and a vodka.'

'What've you got detention for?' I demanded. How come my brother is only back at school for a day and he's already in trouble?

'Kicked a teacher in the head and set fire to the gym. Nothing much really.'

Hmmm, I forget sometimes how much of a wind-up merchant my brother can be. 'Very funny,' I said. 'Have you really got detention or is that made up as well?'

'Nah. It's pouring with rain and freezin' outside, so me and Charlie and Ella offered to help the librarian with this amnesty thingy.'

'Oh, you're doing a thing for Amnesty International... that sounds good,' I said, impressed.

'Yeah, but it's not that kind of amnesty,' Ryan told me. 'It's for library books what people haven't brought back.'

'Library books "that" people haven't brought back,' I corrected him without even thinking.

'Yeah, that's what I said...'

'I suppose that's still a good cause,' I said and my brother sighed.

'It was wet outside, cold and the classrooms are no fun at dinnertime. We just wanted to be warm. Anyway I need to get back before Mrs Scott spots me out here. So spit out whatever it is you got to say, sis.'

'Jane got a call from the hospital,' I told him. 'They think Mum is getting worse.'

'So why didn't they ring you, sis? She's our mum, not Jane's!'

'I don't know,' I told him truthfully. 'I guess coz she's your foster carer and... Well, they probably just forgot I existed. Jane told them off for not contacting me. Anyway, it seems that Mum is drifting in and out of consciousness coz she's still eating so little and she's not drinking much either. She still thinks everyone is trying to poison her. Her heart's not that good since the overdose thingy and they worry... Well, they worry she might go into a coma or something.'

'So what's new?' Ryan's tone was sharp. He gets dead upset about anything to do with Mum. 'It's not like she even recognises us anyway.'

Last time we visited Mum was convinced that both me and Ryan were from the company that made the computer which she thinks runs her life. She was going on about them wanting to shut her down. They give her loads of drugs at the hospital to stop her getting too upset, but I'm not sure if that really helps or just makes things worse. Mum was always strange but she's changed a lot since she got the extra brain damage from that overdose. I guess they have to manage that as best they can, but you hear these stories about people being so doped up just to make it easier for the staff to manage them. I've asked Jane what she thinks and she really doesn't know. She says that maybe without the drugs Mum would be even more distressed, more paranoid than she already is. I don't like the idea of Mum being terrified all the time, so yeah, I really don't know.

'If Mum goes into a coma she might never come out. We need to think about that, whether we want to see her... just in case.'

'In case of what? In case she dies?' Ryan said. I can hear he's trying to sound like he doesn't care at all, but I can see through all that tough guy stuff he does. Underneath it all he's hurting like crazy, coz he really loves Mum, probably much more than I ever have.

'Yeah, that... but also because it might be the last time she's kind of normal... where there's some chance she recognises us.'

'She never recognises us,' Ryan said bluntly.

'She recognised you a bit one time,' I reminded him. 'She said something about how tall you'd got.'

'Nah. She meant how tall the bloke from MI5 had got – or the freakin' monster from the black lagoon she thinks I am!'

'Honestly Ryan, I saw it in her eyes. She did know it was you. I mean she knew you were her son.'

I remember it well coz Mum hadn't recognised me at all and that had hurt. Not a flicker of recognition.

'Look, don't make a decision now,' I told him quickly, 'Think about it. We also don't have that long – sorry, that's a bit of a mixed message.'

'Yeah, right.'

'And I'm going to try and contact Dad. Jane thinks the agency is bound to have something on their records. An address or phone number or something for him.'

'He's not my dad,' Ryan replied, irritated. 'You do what you like.'

'I know he's not your dad but he always treated you like he was. He never treated you any different from me, even when he knew you knew he wasn't...'

'Yeah and what a freakin' brilliant dad he's been, runnin' off to America and getting other kids and never getting in touch. Anyway, I got to go now coz that Scott woman is around and I can't say I was in the bog forever...'

My brother disconnected. He had a good point. Dad hadn't been in touch for a long time. He used to send cards and letters occasionally but that all stopped after he got settled in America. I have no idea where he lives now coz in his last letter he told me he was moving on and he'd let me know where. He never did, but he's still my dad and he has a right to know about Mum.

It's not like we have any grandparents. Mum's mum died when she was little and her dad was an alkie so she never had anything to do with him. And she always thought he'd died coz she couldn't see him surviving long in that state. And my dad and his brother grew up in a children's home and he never wanted anything to do with his real parents. Then his brother joined the army and they never saw much of each other. I guess it's no wonder that my dad isn't good at being a dad; he's hardly had the best role models for playing Happy Families. But that didn't mean he couldn't learn. I'm pretty persuasive when I want to be and he's going to discover that I'm not a little girl any more. He'll be dead proud to know that I've got into a great art school.

After Ryan hung up I called the agency. I told the woman the switchboard put me through to that I already have a copy of my own records – I applied for them the day I turned 18 – but there was no mention of my dad's details in there.

'Everything would be in your file, dearie,' she told me. 'If it isn't, then we haven't got it.'

'Yeah, but that's not true is it? You have to take out mentions of "third parties" don't you? So somebody took out my dad's contact details before they gave it to me. You've probably got that stuff written down somewhere.'

'If you say so,' the patronising woman on the phone continued. 'You said you used to have some contact with your dad. Maybe you've still got his address written down in an old address book or something, and if he's moved maybe someone there could tell you where he's moved to.'

I told her that I'd only ever had a PO Box address in the States for my dad and anyway my social worker used to pass on his letters – some arrangement that the department had made, coz my mum got all paranoid that Dad was planning to hurt her and the idiot worker she'd had at the time believed this and told social services, who'd decided he might be a threat to us. So "contact" had to be through this letterbox system that some charity ran on behalf of social services.

'Can't you give me the number for those people who ran the letterbox thingy?' I demanded.

'Oh that stopped, a year or two back.'

'And where did their files go?'

'Oh, anything relating to the individual would be placed in the individual's file.'

'Yeah, you've said that before, but the thing is there is no reference to any contact details for my dad in my file. The info's got to be somewhere.'

'You could always make an appointment to come in and see someone... it would probably be the same department who showed you your file. Do you have the number for them? No? Let me give it to you.'

I rang the people who hold the original of my file and had another conversation with someone who asked if I wanted to make an appointment to see someone about my file. I said yes, and she said there was a free slot in early February and I said that was no good coz my mum could be dead by then, and I put down the phone.

I rang to speak to Jane but she wasn't there. Martin answered and I told him all about the maddening conversations I'd had with the people on the phone.

'It's not their fault and I'm not mad with them as people, but I'd like to blow the whole bloody service up at the moment coz I'm that frustrated. It's just that this is my life, my dad, and they've gone and lost a huge chunk of my life and nobody seems to care or feel that they need to do anything about it.'

Martin listened to me rant for a bit and made soothing noises. Then he said, 'What about that social worker you had? Ahmina, wasn't it?'

Why hadn't I thought of her before? If anyone was going to lose something it was bound to be Ahmina. She was the most disorganised social worker I knew. OK, it turned out that someone in her family had been really ill and she was on the verge of a breakdown coz her husband was losing his job, and they had to sell their posh house and move away – or that's what I heard from this girl I know who also had Ahmina as her worker...

But just as I thought about Ahmina another name came into my head: Donald. He'd been my brother's social worker when he lived in Newcastle and he'd been totally brilliant. If Ahmina was an example of a not so good social worker, then Donald was probably the best you could ever find. He was just the kind of person who'd bother to find out everything that mattered about a kid and keep records, even if they were about a step-father who nobody else seemed to think mattered very much. Donald doesn't always do everything by the book like some people do.

I got Martin off the phone as quick as possible, although it seemed only fair to let him tell me about how he was learning to make really fancy flaky pastry, coz he seemed dead excited about it. I said I couldn't wait to taste it but I had to go coz I was nearly at work.

I rang Donald during my break. I've had his number in my phone since the days my little brother used to do his running away stuff. Every now and then I send Donald a little text just to tell him how I am and how Ryan is getting on. I know that's probably not allowed coz Ryan isn't his "client" any more, but I was never Donald's "client" so I guess that kind of lets him bend the rules. He always texts back, even if it's just to say, 'Good to hear from you Holly. How's your study going? You painted a masterpiece yet? Don't forget to invite me to your first gallery opening!'

And I think he'd come if he could. If he wasn't busy saving some kid from a horrible situation or listening to some kid who really needed to be listened to, or sorting out some problem that nobody else could even begin to think about... or any of the other things Donald does so brilliantly.

I got Donald's answerphone which is normal. I tried to make my message as short as possible and sent him a text to tell him I'd left him a message. He probably won't get back to me for a few days but I know he will, coz he's Donald and he always does.

FRIDAY 9 DECEMBER

Busy evening at the garden centre. The Christmas rush is hotting up and Marje offered me extra to go in, coz she was short-staffed. One of the new girls has discovered she's allergic to tinsel or something, although it's more likely to be a plant coz you can sometimes get a bit of a reaction when you handle some of them for the first time. Her mum insisted she couldn't come to work any more and gave Marje a major lecture on health and safety, and accused her of being a bad employer and threatened to call the council and complain. Marje and I agreed that some people have too much time on their hands. And she even told me that she's authorised my extra payment for painting the gnomes. I did wonder whether she would but I think she feels I deserve it for all the hard work I've done for the centre during the year. I'd never go off just coz my hands got a bit itchy from something.

Oh yeah, the flowers from Sean arrived today and they are nice. The buds are so delicate and fragile, but also strong coz of the way their petals grow so densely together. And they have such sharp thorns. Hmmm... I wonder why Sean chose roses for me ☺.

I ought to thank him before I go to sleep. It would be kind of rude not to, but I'm so tired, Diary. I've slogged like a worker ant today! I think it can wait till tomorrow.

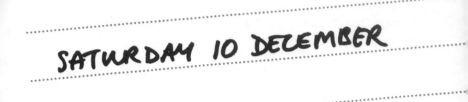

SATURDAY 10 DECEMBER

Davina loves the jacket! I'm so relieved. I was kind of worried that I hadn't heard from her but I had so many things to think about yesterday, so I didn't let it get to me. She rang to say she was sorry but they'd had a bit of a crisis with a lost delivery and she'd forgotten to tell me how much she liked it. She's also agreed to pay me the amount I was asking. She has a client who she knows really goes for my clothes and she's going to give her first refusal. If not, the jacket will go on the rail and she's sure someone else will want it pretty quickly. Davina is so brave about what she sells and I admire that in her. Lots of boutique owners would go for a set number of suppliers and buy everything from them, but Davina is passionate about getting really unusual and unique stuff. She often goes off to Rome and Paris buying new stock and she also buys from some other local designers like me (except they produce more designs than I do coz they've got a proper business set up and I just sew in my bedroom). I guess Davina has the money to take risks and she has the boutique coz she loves clothes. It's not just a business to her, it's her lifeblood. That's why Keesh works for her; she says every day is different and she's learning so much.

Davina might be a dragon some days but she's a pussycat on others and she does pay for Keesh to go on courses and personal development stuff, and even sometimes takes her along to important meetings.

Guess what, Diary! Lucy is going on a date. She texted me to say that she's agreed to meet this Aiden guy from the party. They're going to a film she's seen advertised on TV that everyone says is good. Apparently she wouldn't be going if it wasn't something she really wants to see. She's also going because she doesn't want to disappoint him coz he's been "very sweet". Anyway it doesn't really matter coz it means she's going out somewhere, seeing other people and not sitting indoors staring at her four small walls.

SUNDAY 11 DECEMBER

I did a long day at the garden centre and I'm dead knackered.
I ended up helping out in the café coz the cook walked out
yesterday after an argument with Marje over wages.

I rang Jane this evening to say I definitely want to see Mum on
Wednesday, whether or not Ryan wants to. But I really think he
should. Jane thinks so too and she's going to have a proper chat
with him at bedtime. She thinks he's got a lot of anger inside him
at the moment and he's turning it towards Mum coz he feels she's
failed him so much. Like he felt Susanna failed him, although that
was only in a small way. I hope he doesn't feel I've failed him. I've
always tried to be there for him, whatever trouble he's been in.

Jane asked if I want her to come with me to see Mum. She
comes with us normally coz Ryan's fostered by her and it helps him
if she's there. But she doesn't have to come with me, coz I'm an
independent adult. Still, I like it that she asks and I say, 'Yes, yes
please' because Jane is always good with Mum and knows how to
handle things. Much better than I do.

MONDAY 12 DECEMBER

I woke up to a text from Jane saying that Ryan definitely doesn't want to come with me to see Mum. She said he didn't even want to talk about Mum and she didn't think there was any point trying to force the issue. Jane said she would mention to him that she was coming with me, so he could change his mind although I guess that's not going to happen. She also said did I mind giving her a hand with wrapping parcels after the visit coz she's getting behind and she's got loads of stuff to do before they fly to Lapland? I said sure, I would help. So we can wrap them together, to keep the boys from peeking, which means Martin as well because he's a bigger baby than Si or Ryan when it comes to presents. He has the wrapper pulled off a prezzie faster than any kid I know. Shame really coz it's often only a pair of socks. I think Martin actually likes getting socks but he's always especially thrilled when it's chocolate. This year I'll get him the biggest box I can afford.

Jane also suggested I stay over tomorrow night so we can go to the hospital together on Wednesday. I rang the hospital to tell them we're going and they said that was good, coz Mum is getting even weaker.

Got a text from Sean as well, asking if the flowers ever turned up. Damn. I meant to thank him. He sounds a bit hurt or miffed, or maybe both. I felt guilty and lied:

yeah they fab. Dint u get my txt to say they arvd? Big hug Hols

He texted back to remind me he's coming home tomorrow. He had to hang about in London for a few days after term ended coz he had an interview and photoshoot with some indie music mag and he's only got one spare day before the family flies. But he says he can't go without seeing me. I said sure, but I had to work so I couldn't see him for long.

OK Diary, I have to be honest. I'm still dead miffed with him about Australia. I just hate the way his mum always gets her own way about everything and she always seems to come first. If he really loved me, wouldn't he say no to her sometimes? He's had his mum all his life and she's had him, and this Christmas I was going to get a bit of him too. But oh no, Holly Richards doesn't matter coz she's only some girl from care and that makes her a second-class citizen in his mum's eyes.

And... Yeah, I can't believe I'm going to confess this, but Diary I have been thinking about Tol a bit. Not in a romantic way or anything coz I definitely don't have feelings for him, even if his eyes do still do weird things to me, but it's just that I kind of want to talk to him. He messed with my head and he messed with my little bro's life, and I want to know why he thought he had a right to do that. But it's made me think that maybe all boys are rubbish and you can't rely on any of them. Except Dan, maybe, but Dan's a friend and that's different.

I wanted to say this to Lucy when she texted and asked what I thought she should wear to go to the cinema. But I didn't coz I am glad she's going out and having a life. I said she always looked good and she shouldn't make too much effort if she doesn't want this boy to think she's really keen. She texted back to say she doesn't really like him and she's not sure why she's going. Yeah, very likely. Lucy had her pick of boys that evening, so why would she be going with this guy if there wasn't something she liked about him?

Some days I wish I was like Mum and believed my life was controlled by someone else. Today it would've been good if someone pressed the remote control and switched me off. Not for ever but just for 24 hours, so I could hibernate or something, and the whole crazy world could get by without me for a day.

It was the last day of college and all the students were wanting to hang around for ages over just one cappuccino, all chatting and chilled and gossiping about their Chrissie plans. And we have this stupid tape of Chrissie songs that management says we have to play in a continuous loop. It really does your head in when you've heard it 100 times. It was like everyone was dead jolly except me. I was the grumpy barista with the sewn-on grin. I felt all hyped up and jumpy. Every tiny thing got on my nerves. Then this girl managed to bump into this guy carrying a tray and six cups of coffee went all over the floor and there was this lake of milk and broken china and dissolving sugar packets, and all the sticky stuff from the flavoured syrups. Not to mention the pastries and donuts gently dissolving in the middle... And guess who spent the next 15 minutes on her hands and knees clearing it all up! Kerry said she'd help me but I said no, I was fine doing it by myself. You don't have to smile and be nice to bits of broken china and I got to take some of my frustration out on the floor cloth.

I heard my phone going while I was finishing the mopping up but I had to wait till my break to get Donald's message. I rang him back straight away.

'Holly, how you doing?' his voice was full of warmth and friendliness, the good old Donald I remember. 'Sorry to hear your mum's been taken so bad. Tell me about it.'

So I told him about it. And I told him, too, about my frustration in trying to track down my dad's details. How I'd tried FB and internet searches and there were loads of people with my dad's name but nobody who seemed to be him.

'They want me to make an appointment, probably so someone can then contact my dad and ask him if it's OK for me to have his address or phone number or something, which could take months because I'm not sure if they really know where he is and I don't have months. Mum could die any day... '

'I can see that, Holly. It must be very frustrating. There's no point in my telling you that's what the guidelines say they have to do, because strictly speaking we're not allowed to give out third-party information.'

'Yeah, but he's my dad!'

'Unfortunately they will probably say that if he wanted you to have his mobile number he'd have requested that it was given to you,' Donald explained, but not in that patronising way some people have when they're telling you stuff you don't really want to hear. Donald always speaks to people with respect and he always gives you reasons if he can't do something. That's what makes him so brilliant at his job.

'Yeah, I know all that stuff,' I said. 'But I want to let him know that Mum is dying because...' I stopped because I realised I didn't really have a reason.

'Because?' Donald asked me kindly. 'Why do you feel you need to do this, Holly?'

'Honestly? I don't really know. I mean it's not like he's going to jump on a plane and fly straight over. He probably doesn't want to see Mum again, coz she made his life hell.'

'But is this about your mum, Holly? Could it be... just maybe this is about you needing to know your dad is still there for you, especially if your mum might not be around much longer?'

Clever Donald. He'd put his finger right on it. 'Yeah,' I said. 'I think that's absolutely it.'

'And have you told the agency this: that you urgently need to contact your dad because your mum is dying and you really want to be in contact with your dad?'

'Well, not exactly. I mean I didn't think it was really their business. He's my dad and I think I have a right to his number.'

'Sure. I understand that Holly but it isn't me you need to convince. May I suggest – if you don't mind me saying this – that you get back on the phone to the agency and explain the full situation? Tell them that you really want your dad to know what's happening; tell them that you badly want to have contact with your dad at this difficult time. Then tell them that you want them to contact your dad in the States as a matter of urgency.'

'Thank you,' I said, because when Donald put it like this I could see that was probably going to be the quickest way of doing things.

'And if you're wondering if I have a phone number for your dad and if I'd give it to you... Well, I do have a number which I had on Ryan's files, but I guess it's the one you had for him before. If you read me what you have, we can compare.'

Donald is very good at being helpful without directly breaking the rules.

'Sorry Hols, that's the one I've got. I never actually had any direct contact with him. But I do have a note here about where he worked. Would that be any good?'

'That would be brilliant!' I said. 'It's possible he still works for them and they could get in touch with him faster than the agency.'

Donald spelt out the name for me – CommuniCore – and it rang a bell. I remember Dad mentioning it once in a letter.

'You doing anything nice for Christmas?' I asked Donald, remembering my manners.

'Well, actually I am,' Donald told me. 'I'm getting married, Holly. Some foolish woman has agreed to settle for an old codger like me.'

'Wow! Congratulations!'

I had a vague memory of Donald mentioning an ex-wife but I've always thought of him as a loner, someone married to his work.

'My wife-to-be is from Portugal and we're flying out at the weekend, for a quiet little family wedding in her home town. My children are coming too, with their families.'

I'd never imagined Donald having children of his own. That was quite a surprise to me.

'Is she a social worker too?' I couldn't resist asking the question, suspecting I already knew the answer.

Donald laughed. 'Am I that predictable, Holly? Well, actually she isn't... she was for a long time, but these days she runs her own business, making hats.'

'What kind of hats?' I asked, genuinely intrigued.

He told me a little about his wife's hat business. She made quite funky ones by the sound of it. It was really strange hearing Donald talking about something that was nothing to do with children or young people, and rather nice. I like to think of Donald having a life. But it also made me a bit sad. I wasn't sure why.

Before we hung up, I asked Donald for his office address so

I could send a wedding card. I know he's not allowed to give me his personal address so I didn't ask, coz I knew he'd feel awkward having to explain why he couldn't. He told me to let him know how I got on with tracking my dad. And he said he hoped my mum was going to be alright. I said I hoped so, too, but I wasn't expecting much. I wished him a happy Christmas and a brilliant wedding day and he said he wished me all the good things I deserved. I shed a tear when the call was over.

Dan met me in the café, soon as his lectures were over. I was nearly done and Kerry said I could go early coz we'd had such a crazy day. She said she owed me one for covering when she was off with flu. Kerry's dead nice, I've never got to know her properly coz she's my manager and she's older than me, but hey, I'm going to make more effort to chat to her next time we work together. She's so much nicer than the miserable bloke who was here before Kerry got the job.

Dan guessed something was wrong coz he said my texts weren't as perky as normal. That boy knows me too well. He didn't even ask me anything, he just put his arm round me and waited to see if I wanted to talk. I found that I did, coz sometimes sharing things really helps, and Dan is a good listener. He also looked up the details for CommuniCore on his phone and bingo, they were still trading. And he checked the time in the USA and it was morning there, so he just went ahead and rang up head office – before I could have second thoughts about it. He put on this posh English accent and asked how he could contact a friend of his called John Richards, who worked for them. Dan put his phone on speaker so I could hear the receptionist saying would that be the English John Richards, and if so he was now at the New Jersey office, where he was deputy head of division.

Dan said something like 'Good old Johnnie, always knew he'd go far,' in that really crusty English voice that you hear in black and white films, and the receptionist giggled like a schoolgirl on the end of the line. And she gave Dan my dad's office number! And his business email address as well.

'You be sure and tell his PA that you're a friend of his,' the receptionist told Dan. 'He's sure a very busy man and he gets lots of calls and well... hey she can be a bit of a rottweiler, if you get my meaning...'

She was right about the rottweiler stuff. It must be easier getting to speak to Barack Obama! Her boss was in an all-day meeting and wouldn't be available. And when I wasn't prepared to explain any details about what I wanted to speak to Mr Richards about, she was very unhelpful. In the end she grudgingly agreed to pass on my name and telephone number. 'Will he know you?' she barked at me from the other side of the world.

'Yes, he'll know me,' I said.

My meeting with Sean was a bit of a disaster. There was an accident on the line and his train was delayed by nearly five hours, so instead of getting in by midday he wasn't here till late afternoon. He had to allow enough time to pack his suitcase and I was going over to J and M's for supper, so neither of us had a lot of time. I met him at the station and we sat in a coffee place, drinking watery hot chocolate and being edgy with each other.

Sean had a neatly wrapped present for me and a really beautiful card of a painting he knows I love, and that made me feel awkward. I had planned to leave most of my shopping till Christmas Eve coz I wanted to make sure I'd earned everything I could and anyway, some of the shops start reducing stuff then as they think they might not sell it. But I'd forgotten that Sean wouldn't be around, which is a bit rubbish given that he's my boyf. I could at least have got him a nice card. He said it didn't matter but I could tell he was a bit upset.

He wanted me to open the present and I asked please could I

leave it for Christmas Day coz I love having things to open on the day itself. One Christmas me and Ryan were with these short-term foster carers who didn't celebrate Christmas and I wished so badly I'd had a present from my mum or some school friends or something to open, so I have a bit of a thing about keeping stuff till the day itself. He said that was OK coz I'm sure I've explained to him before why I do that, but again I could see he was disappointed. I think he'd got all excited about seeing my face when I opened it and maybe it was a bit mean of me to deny him that.

He'd also brought a card for J and M and Lucy, and there were little presents for Ryan and Si and Ruby. 'I don't have many kids in my family,' he said, 'and I'm a big kid at heart, Hols.' But I knew it was really coz he cares about my family and he'd made an effort. Unlike his skanky girlfriend.

We didn't mention his mum at all. Instead I asked a lot of questions about the flight and where his relatives lived and what the temperature would be like when he got there. I hoped he would think I was interested. He answered them all a little bit as though he was embarrassed and kept trying to ask me questions about how work was going and stuff that mattered to me. But it all felt a bit awkward, like we couldn't connect properly. I think it was because of the Elephant in the Room – his mum – who neither of us was going to mention. But he did ask about my mum and tell me I could contact him anytime. He said he didn't want me to spend a lot of money so best to use FB or Twitter and send DMs. I told him that never feels secure to me coz of stuff that's happened to my brother, and he said that I could always email him if I really needed to tell him private stuff.

I was kind of glad when he said he really had to go. But he did pull me into a big hug and when he kissed me there were definitely some fireworks going off. But then just as I was wanting a lot more, he pulled away from me to catch his bus. I watched him run across the station concourse and I felt like crying.

I was glad I was staying tonight with J and M. Ryan was staying round at the twins' house. Lucy was out on her date, so me, Jane, Martin and Si had pizza from the takeaway. Then me and Jane went into a huddle with wrapping paper and sellotape while Martin put Ruby and Si to bed.

Now it's time for my beauty sleep.

middle of the night — J and M's

I just got woken up by Lucy clattering up the stairs and telling Boots not to purr so loudly. She's obviously had a good night out.

In a way it was good she disturbed me coz I was having this dream about Tol. I hate the way you don't have any control over dreams. I dreamed about that time when me and Tol went to Cambridge for the day and we took this boat out on the river and we made love in the grass. It was so good back then coz I didn't know what he was really like and I was crazy about him and I think he was crazy about me. And I'd waited so long for the Right Boy and I definitely thought he was The One.

In the dream he was holding me and looking in my eyes and saying, 'Whatever happens, Holly, I will always love you,' which was rubbish coz he never said that and if he had it would have been a lie anyway. If he'd really loved me he'd have stuck around after Ryan took the overdose, not run off like a pathetic, scared rabbit. But in the dream I believed him and I was feeling so lucky to be with him, and Sean didn't exist at all so I had nothing to feel guilty about.

WEDNESDAY 14 DECEMBER

11.45pm

What can I say about the visit to Mum? Ryan didn't change his mind about not coming, and I understood that. Everything was much the same as when I went last time. The hospital staff try to keep the room looking bright and nice and to cover up the smell of disinfectant. But the place has this whiff of something very depressing – maybe it's the smell of sadness, or a feeling of despair. Mum still had the same room to herself with her own little bathroom. And she hadn't changed at all, except she was even thinner. So thin she was almost a skeleton.

The nurse I spoke to beforehand told me what to expect. Mum hasn't been eating for months because she's so convinced that "They" (MI5 or terrorists or whoever she's scared of at the moment) are trying to poison her. The hospital staff have been trying to feed her by tube. They have to do that because legally when someone is as confused as Mum, they aren't considered to be making sensible decisions and the law requires them to be kept alive.

Jane said she got the impression that "reading between the

lines" the staff thought feeding her by a tube was doing more harm than good. She was getting even more frightened and didn't trust anyone any more. And she often vomited up the food as soon as they got it into her. But the hospital directors said it had to be done coz the courts would insist. They'd probably be considered "negligent" if they didn't.

I said I thought it was crap. If Mum is so unhappy then what's the point of making her even more unhappy by forcing food down her? But she's also my mum and I really don't want her to die, and I still hope that maybe one day she will go back to being who she once was. Although I know that's not likely to happen. I'm kind of conflicted on this one.

I walked into Mum's room expecting the worse but the worse is always somehow a bit worse than I expect. Maybe it's coz she's my mum and mums should be like Jane – solid and real and sensible – and my mum is nothing like that at all.

'You've got visitors, Brenda,' a kind looking nurse told the huddled figure on the bed, as she ushered us towards two chairs. Then she left us alone, closing the door quietly behind her.

It looked like there was a small child under the covers. No, not even a child, just a bundle of sticks. Mum seemed to be sitting up but kind of hunched over, and she had the blankets pulled up over her face. She was holding the edges with two claw-like hands with filthy nails, and her hands were shaking.

'Hello, Brenda,' Jane said, 'We've brought you some flowers.'

Bless her, Jane brings flowers every time. I think it makes her feel like she has something to do. Jane knows her way round Mum's little bathroom quite well and she even brought in a vase for Mum to have as her own. She put Mum's name on the bottom so nobody would take it away.

I don't think anyone else visits Mum or ever brings her flowers, coz she never had many real friends. She was good at driving people away, being difficult with people who were doing their best to help her, asking a bit too much when they couldn't take any more. So everyone dropped out of her life eventually, including my dad. The hospital told me once that the hospital chaplain comes in to see her and sometimes the volunteers who visit people who don't have family or friends. I wonder if Mum greets them any better than she sometimes greets us? Does she scream at them, imagining they've been sent by the Queen to kill her?

Jane had suggested I bring my costume for the masked ball with me, so I could sit and sew. 'Better than just sitting and looking at her, and less pressure for her,' she'd explained when I asked if that was maybe a bit rude. So I got on with some intricate detail I'm doing on the bodice and as I was sewing I found myself talking. 'This is a dress I'm making to go to a ball, Mum,' I told her. 'I make dresses for this woman Davina and she's having this big masked ball on New Year's Eve. I was going with my boyfriend but he's away in Australia, so I'm just going on my own with my friend Keesh, or maybe my friend Dan, if his girlfriend Rani will let him come with me. The main reason I'm going is coz I want people to see what fabulous clothes I make, so I get lots more orders to sell my dresses.'

I babbled on for a bit and I noticed that the figure on the bed seemed to be listening. It was hard to tell, coz she went on clutching the covers to her face.

Jane came back with the flowers and sat in the chair on the other side of the bed. When I ran out of stuff to tell Mum, Jane started telling her about Ryan. How he was doing at school, about him being made football captain and how he was showing an interest in a career in drama or performing arts. Jane told her how funny Ryan could be and the stupid practical jokes he played. She didn't mention anything about the moody, angry boy my brother had been recently. She even told Mum about the forthcoming visit to Lapland. And she just went on chatting in this friendly way, though all the time she was talking to this person who was clutching a blanket in front of their face.

'To be honest, Brenda, I have no idea why we're going. It couldn't be at a worse time of year. I'm so disorganised with presents and parcelling, and I've hardly done any of the food shopping, and my eldest son Rob and his wife and the three boys are all coming, and they always eat me out of house and home, not to mention Ryan and Simon.' Jane spoke to Mum like she was an old friend, like she was confiding in someone she really trusted. I was dead impressed that Jane could do that. I think the stuff I told Mum sounded a bit false, like I was having to make a big effort.

'Have I told you about Simon? I think I may have done,' Jane continued. 'He's 10 years old, another of our boys – totally different to your son Ryan but they're good lads, both of them. You should be very proud of Ryan – and Holly too. Holly is such a star. Do you know she's got a place at a really good art school in London?'

I was blushing as Jane described me. She told Mum that I was brilliant to have got not just one part-time job but three; that the garden centre would probably close down without me, that I made the nicest cappuccino she'd ever tasted and that my clothes were the best things in Davina's boutique.

As Jane talked, the figure on the bed became quieter, the hands stopped shaking so violently. Then an orderly came in. She looked surprised to see us. 'Time for your programme, Brenda,' she said, nodding at the TV. 'But I see you've got visitors. I'll leave it, shall I?'

The hands came down and I saw the face behind the covers – wizzened, lined and so old looking. The eyes had a hopeless, dead look to them. Her hair, which used to be as thick as mine, was thin and wispy, and there were some pink, bald patches on her head. The cracked lips opened and a hoarse voice whispered, 'Put it on.'

The orderly switched on the TV and Mum's whole attention was focused on the set. It was like me and Jane weren't there any more. We left quietly after a few minutes, murmuring our goodbyes, and she just stared at us for a couple of seconds, barely registering us at all. I realised half way down the corridor that I still had Mum's Christmas present in my handbag, a selection of bathroom smellies. I decided to keep it, give it to someone else. Someone who knew I existed.

'I can't see how she can keep going. She's going to die soon, isn't she?' I asked Jane, as we drove away.

'Probably. But I suppose it depends whether they can get her to eat.' Jane sounded upset too. She has a very tender heart.

'Yeah, but she's not really there any more, is she? It's like her mind is somewhere else, already gone somewhere too far away for anyone to reach.'

Jane nodded, her eyes firmly on the road, but I could see she was thinking. 'Maybe that's best for her just now. Your poor mum's been scared for such a long time that someone is controlling her life. Remember how she used to say that someone was going to switch her off one day? Maybe she's made her own decision now, that she's the one who is going to do the switching off... and she's started that process of... Well, whatever the process is.' Jane was struggling to find the right expression.

'Downloading,' I said. 'Downloading. Maybe that's what Mum is doing now. Letting go of everything, so she doesn't have to operate any more.'

'Yes,' Jane said. 'I think that may be what she's doing.'

We both cried silently for a bit until I turned on the radio and we sang along to some silly Christmassy songs.

Jane persuaded me to stay over and have supper, and see Ryan. I think she thought he might want to ask me about Mum, but when I reminded him Jane and I had been to see her he just shrugged in a "What's that to me?" kind of way, and he was dead spiky all evening.

Martin had cooked one of his special new dishes: this flaky filo pastry with lots of chunks of meat and gravy and vegetables inside, and it was dead tasty. A bit like a steak and kidney pie but posher. Ryan didn't say anything at all, just pushed the food around his plate, which isn't like him coz he's normally such a piggy. Jane didn't make any comment coz she knows Ryan too well. She was telling me and Martin and Lucy about some new foster carers she's been helping to train, who were beginning to annoy her a bit.

'Third meeting and this man still hasn't got the difference between adoption and fostering. I don't really think he's committed but Julia insists that we have to give them all a proper chance. Personally, I think his wife wants to do it and he's only going along coz he got made redundant a while back. That just isn't fair to children and young people who could get placed with them,' Jane told us passionately.

'Anyway, I don't know how many times I've told him that fostering and adoption are different things. I'm getting a bit sick of explaining that fostering is when you care for someone else's children, like an aunt or uncle or caring for your friend's children, but adoption is when the child becomes a legal part of your family. Honestly, what's so hard to understand about that? Or am I missing something? Do tell me if you think I'm...'

'Yeah, but what about me?' Ryan butted in. 'I mean you guys foster me but you still say I'm part of the family.' His tone was sulky, like he was ready to pick an argument.

'OK. Point taken. You're right. I probably haven't expressed it very well,' Jane said. 'I suppose I should say that it's not that you don't want the child to be part of your family when you foster them. It's just that you need to respect that they already have a family of their own – and that many fostered children will go back to their own family eventually. You need to acknowledge that difference.'

'But what if they're long-term fostered like me and Holly? An' you have some kind of order thingy for them?' Ryan demanded. 'Where does that leave kids like us? I just think this adoption stuff is a load of rubbish.'

Immediately we all looked at Si. He'd been so proud of the fact that J and M have adopted him. His poor little face was a mixture of hurt, scared and bewildered feelings.

'Bein adopted is special,' he murmured in a voice so soft it was little more than a whisper.

'Yes, it is special,' Jane put out a reassuring hand to Simon, aware that he might burst into tears at any moment.

'No it isn't,' Ryan insisted. 'If it's special, that means me and Holly aren't special. Because we're not adopted.'

'It's not quite that simple, is it?' Jane said, her eyes still on the fragile little boy at her side, whose top lip was quivering. 'Adoption was "special" for Si because he really needed a new family. You didn't need a new family, Ryan, because you already have your own.'

Si's birth family are such horrible, dangerous people. A child had already died in their family and then some of his relatives had killed Nathan. They aren't like most people's birth families who try but get things a bit wrong sometimes.

'Yeah, and a lot of bloody good my family are too,' Ryan snapped.

'Thanks a lot, brother,' I said. 'Don't forget that I'm part of your "family".'

'As if I could!'

'Everyone finished?' said Jane, standing up to collect the plates. I knew she was trying to create a diversion.

'My mum's a vegetable and my dad's a loony bastard but that doesn't make me "good enough" to be adopted,' Ryan continued. 'Funny that, isn't it?'

Martin took a long mouthful of water from his glass and looked at Ryan thoughtfully. 'You know that's not how it works, Ryan mate. You and Holly are part of this family, as far as Jane and I are concerned.'

'Yeah, you are,' Lucy looked up from feeding mushed up veggies to Ruby to add her bit. It was the first thing she'd said all meal. She seemed a bit vague and disconnected. She was all flushed and red cheeked and gulping down Diet Coke like it was going out of fashion. I guess she was still suffering a bit of a hangover from her night out. 'You and Hols are like a real brother and sister to me,' she said.

But nothing was going to calm Ryan down. I could see he was working himself up. 'So why is Si adopted then, if me and Hols can just become "proper family" without it?'

Si looked as if he was going into meltdown. Jane quietly placed a miniature dinosaur on the table in front of him. She must have had it in her pocket. I guess she keeps them for these difficult moments. He touched it tentatively with a finger, momentarily distracted, but there were still tears in his eyes.

'Si's situation is different,' I snapped at my thoughtless brother. 'He's younger and needed more security. You know that! Now drop it, coz it's not fair on Si.'

Ryan jumped to his feet, upsetting his water glass which fortunately was almost empty. 'Yeah well, I'll tell you what's not fair, that kids don't get adopted coz their foster carers want to keep getting money to keep them!' These last words were flung over his shoulder before he slammed his way out of the door. I heard his feet as he ran up the stairs.

I stood up to follow him but Jane put her hand on my shoulder. 'Leave him a minute or two Hols. Let him cool down. Don't let him ruin your meal.'

I sat down, feeling so ashamed of my brother. J and M didn't have to take him in but they did because they knew I wanted him to be near me. I hated it when he behaved so badly with them. He knows as well as I do that kids of his age don't get adopted, unless there's some really special situation, like they've been living with their carers for years and they've been waiting and waiting to get an adoption order. But Ryan doesn't need adoption because he still has me and Mum. And I can just imagine what Mad Aunt and Evil Granny and Ryan's dad would do if someone tried to adopt him. They'd gone mildly ballistic about the residence order. That was bad enough. And Ryan knows that. He also knows that J and M don't foster him for the money. OK, the money helps them when they have another mouth to feed and pay for all that petrol and stuff. But Ryan gets the same as Simon; he gets kind of an equal amount of clothes and presents and equipment for school and sports, given that Ryan is older and does more hobbies and things. And anyway, I don't think he'd want a new model dinosaur on pocket money days. Both the boys probably get loads more than me and Lucy got, coz there were more kids in the house when we were growing up and money was tighter. So he has no excuse to behave like a spoilt brat.

I told him this when I went up to his room half an hour later, and I explained it was totally unacceptable that he'd upset Si just coz he was feeling peed off with life himself. And he told me I could f*** off. I tried to calm him down but he brushed past me roughly, forcing his way out of his bedroom. I heard his feet thundering on the stairs as he ran down, followed by the slam of the front door.

Martin met me in the hallway. 'It's OK,' he said. 'He'll just be round the corner in the bus shelter. He goes there to smoke. He thinks we don't know about it but you can't do much round here without some nosy neighbour getting involved. I'll take a leisurely stroll and fetch him in before that woman at number 17 decides to call us again.'

'I hate that he's smoking,' I told Martin. 'It's such a stupid waste of money and he's screwing with his health.'

'Yes, it's not something we exactly encourage,' Martin smiled at me, putting on his coat and gloves in a leisurely fashion. He seemed to take an age changing out of his slippers and lacing up his outdoor shoes. 'But in my experience most kids do it at some point. If you don't make too much fuss, they normally get bored and stop. If you make a huge fuss they know it's a great way to wind you up and they find it even more attractive. Anyway, it's freezing out there and Ryan will be more than ready to be found.'

But Martin didn't come back with Ryan for about 20 minutes. I twitched nervously, unable to concentrate on the documentary on zebras that Lucy was watching with Ruby, covering her eyes from the grisly moment when some poor zebra got pounced on and eaten by lions, and uncovering them to show her cute zebra foals bounding around on their crazy long legs. Jane was upstairs settling Simon, who needed even more dinosaur stories read to him than usual.

When Martin and Ryan came back in there was an atmosphere of something between them that I couldn't quite put my finger on. I got the sense that Martin had found a way to get under my brother's skin and get him to open up. Ryan settled in front of the TV with Lucy, and Martin got him a bowl of the sticky toffee pud the rest of us had been tucking into earlier.

Martin gave me a lift home and we had one of our talks. I asked him if he'd mentioned the dog to Ryan and he said he had, but Ryan said that he didn't want one.

'Why's that?' I asked. I thought my brother would've loved a dog.

'Actually he said he'd rather have a kitten,' Martin explained. 'But he wouldn't give me a reason. My guess is that it's the thought of having something that will curl up on his lap, sleep with him on the bed, something warm and fuzzy and soft. He's quite a softy really, your brother, underneath that brash teenage exterior.'

'Yes, like most boys I know. Girls are so much tougher,' I said. 'I think we are stronger coz we think more, talk about our feelings, so we're better prepared to be independent. But dogs curl up on beds too, and some sit on your lap.'

'I don't know if Boots would tolerate a kitten, not at his age. Boots puts up with many things but I think he has his limits. Remember that time Si tried to colour him with food dye? Boots showed him who was in charge! A dog would be different I think. A dog would respect and negotiate with a cat, use some tact, but kittens are into everything,' Martin said.

'Yeah, but sometimes cats are OK with a new kitten. It kind of depends on the kitten. Dan's mum got a kitten and her old cat got a second lease of life.'

'We're not ruling out a kitten altogether,' Martin assured me. 'We just need to be sure this is something Ryan really wants. Of course, Si wants a baby dinosaur but we've had to explain we can't afford one of those!'

'And you need plenty of space for a baby dinosaur, in case they grow,' I said, loving the way I can always have silly conversations with my foster dad. He's such a big kid at heart. 'A dinosaur is for life, not just for Christmas.'

'My thoughts exactly, but you try and tell that to Si. Actually I think he'd settle for the kitten too, but I want this to be something special for Ryan. Particularly if he's finding it hard that we've adopted Si.'

'But Ryan knows he can't be adopted. He's never mentioned it before. It's just one of his things to feel hard done about... coz my little brother always needs to be the centre of attention. I think you need to be tougher with him.'

'Ah, thus speaks the voice of wisdom,' Martin was mocking

me gently and I didn't mind at all. I know he and Jane do value my opinion.

'But how about you Hols, how are you doing?' Martin asked me as we turned into my road.

We were still sitting there half an hour later when Keesh came and knocked on the window. She was coming home late from her church group. Keesh has turned back to her religion since Nathe died. She says it gives her a lot of comfort. 'Hey there,' she said as I wound down the window, 'I was thinking maybe you had some hot date in dat car girl, but It's you, Mr Brennan...'

'Are you saying I'm not your idea of a hot date, Keesha?' Martin leant across me to speak to my flatmate.

'I would never say such a ting, Mr B,' Keesh laughed and batted her eyelids theatrically at him.

'Well, I'm glad to hear it. There was me thinking I was losing some of my boyish charm,' Martin replied. 'I must remember to tell Jane that I was mistaken for someone's hot date.'

'I was just telling Martin about Sean going to Australia. Like you, he thinks I'm maybe being a bit hard on Sean,' I explained to Keesh.

'Yeah, I do think she bein' a bit hard on dat poor guy,' Keesh said. 'Glad you agree with me Mr Brennan. You should see dem beautiful flowers he sent her.'

'Ah, flowers. You never mentioned those, Hollybear. She never mentioned those at all to me, Keesha. I can't help but feel you've been withholding evidence.'

'Yeah, but this isn't a trial,' I reminded them. 'Which is good coz if it was, you two would have me sentenced and executed: "Holly Richards, you must hang by the neck till very very dead for being a tiny bit miffed with your man for desertion during Christmas to be with his cow of a mother"...'

'Sure sure, my heart bleeds. Now I'm goin' in coz I'm freezing my whatsits off out here,' Keesh said. 'You comin' in for a coffee or a hot chocolate, Mr Brennan? Or will Mrs B send out a search party for you?'

'Very nice of you to offer, Keesha, but I'd really better be getting home. As you say, Jane will most definitely suspect me of a hot date, and she'll have the police of seven counties searching for me.'

I gave Martin a big hug and followed Keesh into the house. 'Your foster dad is just the best,' Keesh said, as we were pulling off our boots. 'My foster dad was dead strict, no sense of humour. No way! My foster mum, she ask if I want to go stay with them for Christmas but I said no. You know, girl, I rather boil my head in a bag than do that. She only ask me coz she hear about Nathan and she feel sorry for me. She hardly bother to keep in touch with me since I move out.'

It's not like Keesh to ever moan about anything and she's always said that there's no point dwelling on the past, so I was quite surprised to hear her talk this way. I followed her into the kitchen, switching on the kettle while she got out the mugs and hot chocolate.

'S'not like I live with them for long,' Keesh said. 'They decide they couldn't cope with me and Nathe when we was about 14. My foster mum, she say they needed a break coz they had family comin' from Jamaica fo' Christmas and they sent us to respite foster carers, but we never went back to there. Nathan hated that. He couldn't see why they had to send us away. He couldn't understand why they needed a break. But I knew why.'

'Why? What did you know?' I asked, stirring the chocolate powder into a thick paste with a couple of teaspoons of milk.

'My foster mum, Joycie, she didn't trust her husband around us no more. My foster dad, he was like a pillar of da community, but I saw the way he look at me. It gave me da creeps and I know she saw it too. I don't think they had no more chillen placed after we went. Maybe they took babies or somet'ing but no more teenage girls.'

The kettle boiled and Keesh poured hot water over my carefully prepared mixture. We both took our mugs and stirred and stirred like crazy. Hot chocolate with all milk is so much nicer but this stuff you make with water is way cheaper and goes much further.

'He left her 'bout a year after that,' Keesh continued, sipping at her drink. 'Ran off wiv the minister's wife. He was the lay reader at da same church.'

'You know, that's what I can't understand... you goin' to church when you tell me things like that. So many hypocrites and creeps...' It was something which truly puzzled me.

'Yeah, but dat isn't God's fault,' Keesh told me. And she had a point. 'People is just people. They make mistakes. Anyway, ours is a nice friendly church which don't judge no one. We got this woman minister and she says there is good in all religions and in all people. Whe'ver or not they believe in God.'

I sent an email to Sean this evening. I said I hoped the journey had been OK and that he was having a fantastic time. And I said thank you again for those flowers coz they are looking pretty on my bedside table.

Shouldn't have drunk that hot chocolate so late, specially not after Martin's homemade sticky toffee pudding. Feels like it's all sitting there in the bottom of my stomach and it's never going to get digested, and I bet if I do sleep I will have nightmares.

THURSDAY 15 DECEMBER

8 pm

I rang Dad's office today and that secretary answered again. She
gets on my nerves. She's like some over-protective nanny. Yes, she
said, she'd told Mr Richards that I'd rung. Yes, he'd definitely got
the message that I needed to speak to him. No, she didn't know
when he'd be calling me. No, there was no point in me leaving my
number again because she'd written it down correctly in the first
place.

So I'm going to email Dad instead coz I don't think he has any
idea of how serious this is. Donald is right. I have to tell people
what's happening if I want them to listen to me. I can't just expect
the secretary to understand why I need to speak to my dad if I
don't tell her. But I don't want to tell her anything; I don't want my
dad embarrassed. I hate the thought of that secretary gossiping
over coffee break, saying that her boss had this phone call from
some mad English girl who says she's his daughter and that her
mum is dying. I won't do this to Dad. I'll email him instead, but I
won't say "Mum" – I'll say "Brenda". I'll write it like I'm some friend
of the family passing on news of someone he knows. Just in case

that secretary snoops in his inbox.

Damn... phone ringing...

Nearly bloody midnight!

Where was I, Diary? ...Got interrupted by Lucy calling and a million and one things...

Well, guess who walked into the garden centre today? Only the Last Person in the World I wanted to see.

I was sweeping up in the Christmas tree section coz that boy who puts the trees in the machine that flattens them and puts the netting round them never bothers to tidy up. He's just here for Christmas and he's pretty useless. I told Marje that I don't know why she bothers with him but she says everyone deserves a chance. Yeah, very likely. I remember that time she sacked me coz she thought I'd given her precious son a hard time, when she didn't realise that Sleazebag was even more of a criminal than any of us imagined. Maybe it's coz of him that she's not so hard on staff these days. Or maybe that Christmas tree boy reminds her of Sleazebag when he was younger and not such a scuz.

I put my brush down for a second to fetch some rubbish bags and when I got back, there he was, bold as brass, with the broom in his hand. 'You hold the dustpan and I'll sweep these bits in,' he said. Which means he must have been watching me for a while and that felt a bit creepy.

'I don't need help,' I told him, but dropping my voice coz the aisle was really busy with shoppers all over the place. I held out my hand to take the broom back from him.

'Sure you do,' he said, ignoring my hand and continuing to sweep.

If there hadn't been people around I'd probably have yelled at him, told him to b***** off and leave me alone, but I couldn't do that. The last thing I wanted was any kind of scene.

'Just go,' I said to him. 'I have nothing to say to you.'

'But I have stuff I want to say to you. I really owe you an explanation. And I want to apologise properly,' he told me, all earnest and sure of himself. What a bloody cheek!

I looked around for the boy who does the Christmas trees but of course he's never around when you need him. I couldn't see anyone wearing our green staff sweatshirt anywhere close enough to call someone else over.

OK, I thought, there's no way I can leave this swept up stuff hanging around coz someone will stand in it or slip on it or something, and it's not exactly professional.

'Here, you can hold this,' I said, thrusting a rubbish bag at Tol.

As he reached for it I took the broom away from him. I left him standing holding the bag while I carefully transferred all the broken bits of Christmas tree – and other rubbish and dust from the shop floor – into the dustpan. And then tipped it into the bag he was holding. I must have done it about eight times, except I threw it into the bag really fast, and each time a cloud of dust went up and must have gone in his eyes, which is just what I intended to happen.

To give him credit he didn't say anything, although he knew perfectly well what I was doing. At the end I just snatched the bag out of his hands, picked up the broom and marched away. After I'd thrown it in the bin in the storeroom I made myself very useful helping Rhonda to get down some boxes of tinsel from a top shelf. Then Rhonda needed my help to sort out the contents of some badly stacked boxes which had toppled over. Nobody confessed to doing the bad stacking but I bet it was that Christmas tree boy coz he helped out in the storeroom before the Chrissie trees arrived. Half of these great big sparkly gold and red baubles were smashed and a boxload of cute little donkeys and sheep made from twigs were pretty squashed, and there was loads of other stuff that had taken a right battering. Some Christmas tree lights had also taken a tumble and each set needed testing. We wore protective gloves to do it, so we didn't get our hands cut on any of the broken bits. It wasn't a job any of the boys could've done; it needed people who were careful and patient.

While we sorted, Rhonda wanted a bit of a natter. She's convinced she's a bad mum. She says she must be coz her son left home about six months back after he had a row with Rhonda's new bloke, and now she's having constant rows with her daughter. She feels like she can't do anything right for her. I tell her that it might just be coz her daughter's 14 and she's probably got stuff going on in her life with mates and teachers at school, and maybe someone she fancies who doesn't fancy her. I say Rhonda just needs to be patient and not fret too much. And she needs to listen, coz kids want to be listened to, even if they say they don't. I guess Rhonda isn't the best mum ever but she's definitely not the worst. She tries to get things right for her kids, you can tell that. And I tell her that even kids with brilliant parents get pissed off with them sometimes, coz when you're a kid you've got to have someone to be angry with.

While Rhonda was talking I tried not to think about Tol. I wondered how long he'd wait before he realised I wasn't coming out of the storeroom. I also wondered what was making him do this. Did he really want to apologise? Or had he got some stupid idea in his head that him and me could get back together? He did look at me a bit like he still fancied me, but if he thought I'd ever consider that, he must be totally crazy. You don't nearly almost kill someone's brother and then get to go out with them again – even if you have the cutest, greenest eyes in the world.

There was no sign of Tol when I left at 5.30 but I didn't hang around. I grabbed my coat and headed for the bus stop.

Lucy rang coz she wanted to tell me she's seen her new bloke again. She seems really crazy about him, like he's the only boy she's ever been out with. She says she thinks she might be falling a little bit in love with him and I said wasn't that a bit soon? She got really huffy with me and said something about me just being narked because Sean was away. That really hurt me. I told her so and she said it was time I "got over" myself. I ended the call coz I knew I was going to say something I'd really regret, like how I was sick of her moodiness and how I wished the new narky Lucy would go away and the old Lucy would come back and be kind and sweet and easygoing again.

But then about 20 minutes ago she rang me again and she was crying and saying how much she loved me, and how I'd always be her best friend. And we made up and I said yes, I wanted to hear all about the new bloke, and so she went on and on and on for ages about how fit he was. And then she burst into tears again and said she wished that Nathan was still here and she'd never love anyone like she'd loved him... and I have to confess I switched off a bit and started wondering if maybe Tol thinks he still loves me after all this time. Then Lucy asked me what I thought she should wear to go bowling with this Aiden guy tomorrow and I kind of wanted to scream that I didn't really care, coz I was that knackered after a long day at work. I needed to get this written... So I said the first thing I could think of, before lying that I had to go coz I really needed a wee...

FRIDAY 16 DECEMBER

Did another half-day at the garden centre today. It's getting really busy now and lots of staff have gone off with the flu. No time for painting gnomes but I helped out with the house plants and with the Chrissie decorations, and it was dead chaotic like it always is at this time of year.

Late afternoon I went round to J and M's coz they wanted to show me where the gas meters are and where the water turns off and stuff like that. But most of all Jane wanted a word with me in her office, and she made this big thing of pretending she wanted to show me something so we could go in there on our own. She said Lucy was out with Ruby at this Christmas thingy organised by the mums 'n' toddlers club, Ryan was at some computer group his school ran and Si was up in his bedroom drawing dinosaurs. So we had a bit of private time to ourselves.

'This boy,' Jane said after we'd both pretended I really needed to be reminded where the spare keys were kept (in the bottom drawer of her bedside cabinet). 'What's he like, Holly? You met him at the party didn't you?'

I told Jane that, to be honest, I didn't remember him at all.

'They do seem to be seeing a lot of each other.' Jane tried to sound casual, but I could tell she was concerned. 'Don't get me wrong Holly, I'm delighted she's having a social life again, but well, it all seems a bit serious and a bit soon.'

'Yeah, they do seem to be seeing quite a lot of each other, but as you say, it's really good that Luce is getting out again...' I said, torn between my loyalty to Jane and my loyalty to Lucy.

Jane sighed. 'I'm not sure if it's this boy or just because she's going out more, but Lucy seems to be drinking quite a lot at the moment. I have tried to have a word with her, but she says I'm fussing too much and she's an adult. And yes, I know that young women drink a lot more these days than we did when I was young, but I don't think it's a good thing.'

I said I was sure that Jane didn't need to worry but I don't really know why I said that. I guess maybe I didn't want her to worry. She has so much on her mind with the Santa trip and getting everyone organised and all the end of term stuff, and Simon needing a costume for the school play (he's playing a donkey which the school seem to have convinced him is pretty close to a dinosaur) and Jane having to do some last-minute training because the normal trainer is off sick... And I told Jane that I would keep an eye on Lucy when she was in Lapland and make her do loads of girly and mumsy stuff with me and Ruby. Jane said I was wonderful, but I shouldn't have to feel I was responsible for Lucy because Lucy wasn't my responsibility, and I should call her in Lapland if I had any worries. But she also said she really appreciated knowing I'd be around "just in case".

Martin was doing baked potatoes and beans and cheese, but we didn't have a proper sit-down supper as everybody was coming and going and Jane had to be out for some drinks party that was meant to be a thank you for all the work she does for the council, but she said was really one of the most boring things she had to go to.... So me and Martin ate our supper with Simon, who showed us his drawings and me and Martin said nice things and didn't ask which dinosaurs actually had six legs.

Lucy came in about 8.30ish but she seemed edgy and said that Ruby was tired and she had to get her to bed. When Martin said casually that he was surprised the party went on so long and he'd been expecting her to ring him to come and collect her, she got a bit ratty and said a friend had given her a lift. I'd swear I smelt alcohol on her breath and I wonder if she went to the pub with some of the other mums after the party finished.

My brother arrived just before I was leaving. He'd got a lift back with the twins' dad. He came in, slammed the door and was halfway up the stairs before Martin could ask him if he needed anything to eat.

'He's not been eating with us much recently,' Martin told me, 'but maybe you could take a little tray up to him before you go? He might appreciate that. He's really angry with everything and everyone in this house at the moment.'

'What, more so than usual?' I asked.

Martin gave a small shrug. 'Probably a bit more. Simon seems to be winding him up something rotten at the moment – not on purpose of course, because as everyone knows, young Si lives in a world of his own. But everything Si does or the very few things he says, seem to get on Ryan's nerves. Come to think of it, me and Jane can't do much right either as far as Ryan is concerned. I guess it's an age thing. I don't think 16-year-old boys are known for their tact or tolerance.'

'You and Jane are angels,' I said. 'I don't know how you put up with him.'

'Oh, he's much easier than some of the children we've had, Holly. Don't you remember that boy who smashed the telly three times while he was living here and punched half the stuffing out of the sofa? Poor lad... now he really was angry with the world. And who could blame him? He hadn't had a very nice life.'

'I think he headbutted you as well,' I reminded Martin, but he just shook his head.

'Oh, that was just an accident. He didn't really mean to hurt me... He was aiming for the fridge,' Martin smiled, remembering the Nightmare Boy with kindness. Not something that me and Lucy could ever share. We'd never forgotten how he flushed our make-up and all our bubble bath down the toilet. 'Now do you think Ryan would like some salad with his beans and cheese? Oh, what am I asking? Teenage boys don't eat salad. Or not the last time I looked.'

I thought my brother heard me knock and called out for me to enter, but I was wrong. The look of sheer rage on his face told me I'd caught him doing something he didn't want to be caught doing. At first I thought, 'Aha,' and was about to back out but then I caught a glimpse of something that looked very much like a blade.

'Go away,' he growled at me. 'Freakin' leave me alone.'

But I was worried now and I wasn't going anywhere. 'What's that?' I said, pointing at the penknife which he was trying to slide under his duvet.

'Nothin.' My brother crossed his arms defiantly, his hands tucked under his armpits, but my eyes went immediately to the cuff of his pyjamas and the tell-tale trickle of blood.

'This isn't "nothing"!' I snatched at his wrist and pulled it away from his body. He was almost too startled to resist. I pushed up the pyjama sleeve and took a good look.

There was a fresh cut, about halfway up his forearm. But even more worrying, I saw a couple of other scars closer to the inside of his elbow.

'What's this about?' I demanded. 'How long have you been doing this?'

'None of your business!' Ryan snatched his arm away from me.

'Yeah, like it's none of my business when my brother cuts himself!' I sat down on the bed beside him. 'Do Jane and Martin know about this?'

Ryan gave me one of his "Do you think I'm stupid?" looks.

'OK,' I said, deciding to take another approach. 'Why are you doing this? Please try and help me understand... Coz it's freaking me out big time.'

Ryan didn't say anything. I wanted to shake him. But I also wanted to cuddle him and protect him and stop anything from hurting him, so I put my arm around him.

We sat in silence for a few minutes. Then my brother put his head on my shoulder.

'It hurts,' he said, eventually.

'Yes,' I said. 'I guess it does.'

'Not the cutting,' he said, 'That doesn't hurt really.'

'Do you know why you're doing it?' I asked, hoping my voice was gentle, not too demanding.

'No... Well, maybe. Coz it's... coz it...' my brother gave a huge sigh. 'Coz I might explode if I didn't.'

I think I understood what he was trying to say. I think what he meant was that the feelings are too big for him to cope with.

'What's going on inside?' I said. 'What do you feel inside?'

Ryan just shook his head. 'I don't know,' he said, and I believed him.

Then he grabbed my hand. 'Don't tell Jane, promise you won't tell Jane,' he begged me. 'I will try to stop doing it, but I can't have her watchin' me all the time. I might have to... like do... *something else*.'

'You wouldn't? Ryan, promise me you wouldn't!' All sorts of ideas were rushing through my head. I know that teenage boys can and do kill themselves, and my brother was soon going somewhere very very cold. I had this hideous picture of his lifeless body being found in the snow in Lapland, frozen to death coz he'd wandered off, or just stepped off the edge of some icy cliff. Was this why he'd wanted to go in the first place?

'Promise me you won't do anything stupid,' I was holding his shoulders, I realised I was shaking him. 'Sorry,' I said. 'But please Ryan, promise me you won't...'

'Only if you promise me you won't tell Jane... or Martin, or my social worker.' My brother glared at me with solid, stubborn determination.

I had promised myself once that I would never keep my little bro's dangerous secrets again, but this was too difficult. I know Ryan so well. If he got the slightest hint that someone else knew, he definitely might do something stupid. I just knew that. He's so bloody minded. He'd do it just to prove that he could – and that wasn't a risk I could take. So I made him a promise not to tell and then forced him to promise me he wouldn't do anything silly.

I was just trying to leave J and M's when Lucy appeared, all smiles. She said she'd finally got Ruby off to sleep and she'd been thinking that we never had any BF time together any more, and she knew it was my day off tomorrow and so we could meet for a coffee. I said yes because I was already late for my bus and I wasn't going to miss it. Besides, I wasn't in the mood for any more difficult conversations.

SATURDAY 17 DECEMBER

Horrible night. I couldn't sleep coz I was worrying about Ryan; then when I did sleep I dreamed I was in a plane flying over the ocean and I could see a body lying on a floating lump of ice. There were red stains around the body and I knew it was blood, and that the warmth of the blood was going to melt the ice and the body would fall into the water. The plane was too high up and I couldn't see whose body it was, but I had a horrible feeling it was my brother's. And the air hostess said I wasn't allowed to leave my seat because the seatbelt sign was still on, so I couldn't get to ask the pilot if he could fly lower. I started to scream and scream. I punched the air hostess and some of the passengers grabbed me, and someone headbutted me in my stomach and it hurt so much. Then the air hostess said I was a mad woman who ought to be locked up. The passengers shut me in one of those tiny toilets they have in planes and I couldn't breathe. I started screaming at them to let me out and that my brother was dying. But they said that they would hand me over to the police when we got to Iceland and they would probably put me in prison for the rest of my life.

I woke up hot and thirsty and realised that my period just

started and that was causing the pain in my stomach.

I spent the morning reading some of the books for next term and researching this project I want to do with silk screen printing. Wonder if I could make something like that amazing swirly pattern that Keesh liked so much in Camden? There was a lot of detailed work in the hem. But that would be wrong – copying someone else's work – wouldn't it? Artists should never do that coz it's not fair on the other person, and it's a pretty lazy way to behave. We need to stay fresh and original. I know it's OK if you say you're inspired by someone else, so long as you don't claim it's totally original. I will just have to make something that's inspired by that other stuff but is totally my own – and even better. And hope that Keesh likes it as much.

I rang Lucy to say I wasn't feeling up to meeting her in town this afternoon coz I was in lots of pain and just wanted to stay warm indoors, coz the weather is vile. But Luce said she'd bring Ruby and a pizza round to me. I said it was very icy outside and she ought to be careful with a little person in her care. She said it didn't matter coz Aiden would drive her. She wanted me to meet him anyway. He'd probably pay for the pizza coz he made loads of money. She told me he was a model.

Part of me just wanted to be on my own, I didn't want this Aiden coming round, but then I was also kind of curious to check out Lucy's new boyfriend.

They arrived late and there was a bit of an atmosphere. Lucy came in all smiles and hugs, but Ruby was tearful and very clingy with her mum. Aiden just seemed quite tense. It turned out that Ruby had thrown up in his VW Golf which he'd just had valeted. But Lucy was all giggles and sexy pouts. You could see she was dead keen to keep him happy. She must really like this guy.

OK, I could see the appeal of Aiden. He was pretty fit, with these big smouldering eyes and cute curly blonde hair, but he walked with that I'm-so-masculine-and-muscled-I-can-hardly-move swagger that really irritates me. You could understand why he had got some modelling work for a sports company, although it was clear that this wasn't his full-time job, whatever he'd told Luce to impress her. When I finally managed to cut through the charm and swagger and get Aiden to actually answer a question, I realised that he worked for a second-hand car company most of the time. So that explained the posh wheels. At least he wasn't a drug dealer! Or was he? OMG. Did I really write that? What an awful stereotype. But hey, who says I have to buy into the stereotype? I make up my own mind about stuff and to be honest, this guy doesn't seem quite genuine, somehow...

But to give him credit, he does seem really into Lucy. He could barely take his hands off her. I found myself wanting to say, 'Get a room!' Instead I took Ruby off to show her some crayons and paper I keep in my room, just for her. She drew a beautiful blob of squiggly green and a yellow thingy and managed to crayon over the back of one of my textbooks but I don't mind. I will look at it when I'm in London and remember how cute my god-daughter is. Then she fell asleep on my lap while we sat round the table and she was all snuggly and smelt of clean hair and warm toddler skin.

Lucy was all bubbly and chatty and tucking into the pizza and drinking the rosé wine they'd brought, but Aiden hardly touched a mouthful. He said he needed to keep fit and he doesn't drink coz he has to keep his licence for his job. But he was forever topping up Lucy's glass, like some old fashioned wine waiter. I wouldn't have thought he'd need to get her drunk coz she's all over him ☺. He's clearly getting everything he wants from her in the bedroom department. She'd already told me what a stud he was. Again, too much detail, even from a best friend!

And he doesn't really have much time for Ruby. He almost seems to resent it every time Lucy speaks to her or gives her any bit of attention. It's good that Lucy is so focused on her daughter and doesn't seem to notice that he's got a sulk on. I guess not every man is good with kids. I'm just used to being around Sean who is brilliant with little ones, and nobody was soppier about babies than Nathan. Which makes me wonder, what would Nathan have said about this Aiden bloke? Would he have thought he was good enough for Lucy? Oh, hark at me, they've only been together a short while and it probably won't last that long... Lucy has been known to change her mind about blokes in the past. Nathan was the only guy she really totally and utterly fell head over heels for, and that's coz he was such a lovely bloke. At the end of the day, I think Lucy likes nice men much more than handsome ones. It's just that she's been single for a while and she's enjoying the attention.

I was really glad when they left. I emailed Sean to tell him about Lucy's new boyf. I can tell Sean things I can't tell anyone else but it would still be much better if he was here. I'm not exactly looking forward to housesitting for J and M with Aiden hanging around the place. Sean emailed back to say I should give this bloke a chance... He was probably dead nervous about meeting Lucy's best friend and felt he had to impress me or something. He has a point. I think some blokes do find me a bit scary ☺.

SUNDAY 18 DECEMBER

10.30pm

I can't believe where I'm writing this... And sorry Diary, I'm going to have to staple this scruffy bit of paper inside you. But it's all I've got tonight!!!!!

It snowed today while I was at the garden centre. Not a nice fluffy coat of snow but dribs and drabs that didn't settle. And it was soooooo cold. I was pretty fed up coz I'd forgotten my gloves and scarf. I thought they were in my winter coat but I remember I'd put them in my mac pocket and forgotten to move them back. By the time I realised I'd left them I was halfway to the bus stop and there was no time to go back. Anyway, I didn't think for a minute it was going to be a really bad day. It started all bright and sunny and crisp and nice, one of those days that make you feel glad you're alive even if you're up dead early and you'd rather still be in bed. I always forget that it's often the crisp sunny days that sneak up on you and throw snow out of the sky.

I didn't want to be late coz there was this end-of-term party that some mates from college had organised. It's cool that I still get to hang out with the students even though I'm working... best of both worlds. I'd invited Lucy to come along and I'd said we'd meet up with Dan and the gang for a drink beforehand, which meant it was going to be pretty tight on time. I'd brought my clothes with me so I could change in the pub toilets.

Lucy hasn't met many of my college friends and I thought this would be a good chance. And hey, I've always had this thing about maybe her and Dan getting together coz I think they'd really like each other... Dan wants a girlfriend he can adore and spoil rotten and Lucy really needs a lovely guy she can totally rely on. They've only met a couple of times before and that was round the time that Nathan died and Lucy wasn't looking at any men... But Dan did say he thought Lucy was really pretty... And I know he's not so sure about Rani coz he said she's been almost ignoring him again. He really is starting to think that maybe she's met someone else. Maybe he does have a point.

Besides I wanted Luce to see the college, meet some students and realise what she's missing out on by not going back into education. Nathe used to nag her about that, and she'd probably have done something eventually, but now she uses being a single mum as an excuse not to apply for any courses.

So I was cross when this customer started asking for complicated stuff at the last minute, just as we were about to close the tills. It made me really late and with the ground being quite icy, I wasn't going to risk running to the bus stop. Result: I arrived to see the bus disappearing round the corner. I stood at the stop and swore. The buses come about every 20 minutes, later on Sundays, and I could freeze standing there. My boots were soaked through and my socks were soggy. I could feel my feet turning to ice and as much as I tried to shove my hands into my pockets it wasn't working. I tried not to think about that radio programme I heard about a French explorer who had to have his fingers and toes amputated after he lost his gloves on the mountainside. When they

unbandaged his hands there were maggots living in his fingers.
OK, maybe I was being a bit of a drama queen but I was cold and
miserable and panicking about being late...

The squeal of tyres made me look up to see this car sliding
across the road towards me, totally out of control. For a moment
I thought my number was up coz it was coming straight at me... I
guess the driver took the corner too fast and hit a patch of ice but
at the time I wasn't thinking anything except how to get out of the
way before me and the bus stop got smashed to pieces! I think I
sort of jumped sideways and twisted and lost my balance coz the
ground was too slippery for my feet to land... The memory is a bit
fuzzy, but I do remember falling into this wall behind the shelter,
putting out my hands to protect myself. My knee hit the wall and
I felt the crunch of stone against bone, just as the car crashed
into one of the poles that holds up the bus shelter. I thought for a
minute the whole thing was going to topple...

With a roar the car reversed and then sped off, leaving me
standing there, all shaken up and bleeding. I don't remember
exactly what I shouted at the driver but I know it wasn't pretty!
Unfortunately it all happened too fast. I couldn't even tell what
make of car it was, let alone read the number plate.

My head was spinning with a mix of pain and shock. Falling over
is bad enough but when your body's already half frozen, it hurts
like crazy... I could feel myself about to burst into tears. Or spew
my guts up.

The 4x4 that stopped made me jump. It pulled in alongside the
kerb and someone wound down the passenger window. 'Get in.
You will freeze there. We saw what happened as we came down
the hill...' I recognised the accent but I couldn't place it, and I
couldn't make out the shadowy female figure it was coming from. I
limped towards the window, grateful for any help in my miserable
situation.

Close up, I realised it was Ptolemy's mother – not exactly the rescuer I was looking for! I glanced nervously at the driver's seat and, much to my relief, saw an older man behind the wheel.

'I'm OK,' I said, reluctant to have anything to do with this family. 'I can wait for the bus.'

'No you're not. You have blood pouring from your hands and you're clearly very shaken up. Get in and we will take you to casualty.' The voice was commanding. This was someone used to being obeyed. To reinforce the order she stepped out of the car, opened the door and half led, half hoisted me up onto the back seat.

As the 4x4 moved off, she turned in her seat to hand me a box of tissues. 'Those cuts look painful. You're the girl from the garden centre aren't you, the one who paints comedy gnomes?' There was a touch of amusement in her voice, but she wasn't unkind. 'I'm Christiane, by the way, and this is Dermott, my husband. You know our son, I believe?'

I told them my name was Holly and made some kind of non-committal noise in reply to the question. It was weird, sitting in the back of that massive black car, wrapping my hands in tissues.

'You must report it to the police. People shouldn't get away with things like that,' Tol's father told me, his voice deep and posh, reminding me so much of his son. The irony of his comment made me want to laugh out loud. Had they any idea what their son had done? I doubted it very much.

'I didn't see anything, just the car headlights, so there's not much to tell them,' I explained. 'Look, you really don't need to take me to casualty. Nothing is broken. I've just got a few cuts and scratches. You could drop me at the main bus station in Abbotsfield. I'll be warm and dry there while I wait for the bus home. I really don't want to be hanging round A&E all night. They can take ages to see you and I'm meant to be meeting my friends.

There's a big party tonight...'

'I expect that might be true. The waiting times are abysmal these days.' Dermott sounded like he might have better things to do than provide a taxi service to a stranger.

'Yes, but the poor girl can't go anywhere in that state,' Christiane told him sharply. 'She needs to clean up first, put some plasters on those hands.' It was almost as though I wasn't there at all. I felt very awkward being talked about like that.

'Honestly, I'm going to be OK,' I insisted.

'You can't go anywhere with those cuts unbandaged,' Christiane informed me briskly. 'I have an excellent first aid kit at home and I'm trained in first aid – it's essential when you're working in a war zone. I'm a journalist, by the way, but Ptolemy has probably told you that. Dermott, drive us home. That's going to be quicker than dragging this poor girl all the way to casualty. We can get her patched up and then think about getting to... Where is it you're trying to get to?'

I explained about the party at college and fortunately this took Christiane on a sidetrack. She started asking questions about what I did and I told her about my place at St Martins. Of course she'd heard of it but she wasn't quite as impressed as most people are when I tell them about it. She seemed a bit surprised that anyone would consider art as a career. Were there decent career prospects, she asked, and I said yes, especially if you are really focused and work hard. Which is what I'm going to do. But she didn't seem like she actually believed me. She told me that she'd taught herself photography; there were no courses when she was young. She did law at university, then decided that she was in the wrong profession. She went travelling in Africa and a war broke out. Finding herself in a city under siege, she rang one of the big British newspapers and offered to write them a report and that was how her career started.

Christiane seemed very happy to talk about herself. She told me about how you have to have all your wits about you on a battlefield, how journalists and camera people she knew had been killed or injured, sometimes in front of her eyes. She'd also seen hand-to-hand fighting, people blown up with hand grenades, hospitals full of people missing limbs and eyes and hands and feet... She said you had to know a bit of basic first aid or you would never survive. I imagined she would survive anywhere.

When she declared, 'My work is my life. It keeps me sane,' I said I thought it was so important to have work you really care about. I told her that I'd always known what I wanted and had carefully planned my career.

'You seem like you're a young woman with plenty of determination,' she commented, as the car pulled into a driveway. 'I wish Ptolemy was more like you. He has no determination, that boy, no vision or focus.' She said it with so much contempt, such a lack of respect for her son that for a moment I felt really sorry for Tol. No wonder he had so many problems, growing up with a mother like her.

It was a large house, set back from the road. As we approached a light switched on automatically, flooding the area around the doorway with brightness. I couldn't see much but I could tell it was really old. It had that uneven look to the doors and windows that old houses have, like they've shifted a bit in shape. And the bricks were a bit higgledy piggledy, like they'd been there for hundreds of years. There were fir trees all around and ivy growing up the walls.

'Come inside.' Christiane indicated that I should get out of the car. I followed her into the house while Dermott locked up. My knees had gone stiff during the ride and when I stood on them the skin pulled tight, making them sting like crazy, but I wasn't going to show any pain in front of Mrs Ice Queen.

I stepped into the hall and it almost took my breath away. It was the kind of space I'd always dreamed about owning. It had a really high ceiling with ancient oak beams. At one end there was a beautifully carved wooden staircase leading up to a sort of balcony above. You couldn't see much of the balcony coz it was dark up there. On the walls of the hall there were loads of photographs of faraway places: sunsets over the pyramids, a sandstorm in the desert, tigers basking in the midday sun, market stalls heaped high with brightly coloured spices – a whole world of places I've never seen. I just knew that all those photos were taken by Christiane. She was just the sort of woman to welcome people to her house with her own pictures. There were sculptures, too, carvings from stone and wood and bronze and silver. A magnificent horse reared high above its handler and a graceful woman carried a water pot on her head. There were exotic jars from the other side of the world and musical instruments in shapes you could barely imagine.

At the centre of the room was the Christmas tree. They hadn't bought it from our garden centre, coz it was bigger and better than anything we had in stock. I guess it was delivered on a truck or something. It was decorated in blue and silver, with baubles shaped like perfect tear drops. Very cool and sophisticated and nothing at all cosy and cutesy (I thought of J and M's tree with its jolly santas and rocking horses and snowmen on skis). On the beautiful old wooden dresser there was an arrangement of lilies and branches sprayed with silver, and a few bunches of holly leaves and berries, tied here and there with trailing silver-blue ribbons. It was all so tasteful and arty, it looked like something out of a design magazine.

I must have been standing there with my mouth open, just drinking it all in, so it was a minute before I realised Tol was standing in the shadows on the balcony, looking down at me. As I strained my neck up to doublecheck I wasn't imagining him, I suddenly felt really strange. The ceiling started moving above me and I felt my knees crumple.

It wasn't a serious faint but I was dead embarrassed. I do remember Tol and his dad lifting me and carrying me through to a sofa, and his mum placing a pillow under my head, and a rug over my body. I remember Tol holding a glass of water and encouraging me to take sips.

'Probably the shock of coming in from the cold – after the shock of nearly being run over,' Christiane informed me calmly. 'Nothing to worry about. A natural reaction.'

I struggled to sit up and she pushed me back firmly with a hand. She was incredibly strong for such a slim person. I bet she works out at the gym a lot. 'I need to clean and bandage your hands,' she told me. 'So lie back for now.'

The room I was in looked like a sitting room, but quite a casual one. Not the sort of front room where you'd invite posh guests. The furniture was comfortable and a bit shabby and there was a strong smell of dog. Again, there were loads of photos on the wall but also some quite dark paintings of dogs and horses and dead pheasants. There was also a roaring fire, and it felt dead cosy. The sofa I was lying on felt like really old soft leather.

'I need to tell my friends, they're going to be worried,' I told Christiane.

'Fair enough, but you need to let me patch you up first or you're going to bleed everywhere. The skin is thin on your hands and you've made quite a mess of them.'

Meekly I held out my hands for Christiane to clean. She dipped the cotton wool in something antiseptic that really stung but I wasn't going to let her see me flinch. She then dried them with a towel and put on some lint. On my left hand I'd badly skinned my knuckles and she put on a wad of dressing and bound this round with that plaster tape stuff. But my right hand wasn't so cut and she patched this up with a couple of large plasters. Then she turned her attention to my legs. It looked like a sharp piece of brick had cut through the left knee of my jeans.

While Christiane was cleaning me up, Tol appeared with a cup of tea and a slice of Christmas cake. He looked quite anxious, maybe worried I might say something in front of his parents about before...

'She's hardly going to want that!' Christiane nodded fiercely at the cake.

'I thought she might be hungry,' Tol said lamely.

'Actually I could manage a bit of that cake,' I said, quickly. 'The sick feeling's gone and I'm that ravenous.'

Christiane shut the door firmly after shooing Tol out of the room. 'Men are useless,' she said, without a touch of humour or irony in her voice. 'Can you slide your jeans down a bit, so I can dress your knees?'

I was glad I wasn't wearing my old grey knickers, but Christiane put a rug over my lap so I wouldn't feel embarrassed. She pulled the jean fabric away from my knees in a purposeful, no-nonsense manner. The fabric stuck to blood on my left leg and I couldn't help wincing.

'Sorry, I don't think I'm the gentlest of nurses,' Christiane managed something resembling a smile. 'I've got used to doing things quickly because you never know when the next sniper might appear or a bomb explode... Oh, that is rather nasty, that must hurt.' Just when I'd decided I didn't like this woman at all, she showed me her nicer side.

I rang Dan while Christiane cleaned up my legs. He was full of concern and promised he'd be there to meet up with Lucy. He wanted to know if I would join them later but I said to be honest I just wanted to get home to bed. (I didn't tell him but I kind of liked the idea of him and Lucy getting to spend some time together.)

Then he started fretting about how I was going to get home.
'Where are you?' he asked.

I realised then that I didn't have a clue where I was. I'd got
into the car feeling a bit dazed and I hadn't really concentrated on
where Tol's dad was driving.

Christiane couldn't help but listen in: 'Chorsley – you're in
Chorsley. It's about seven miles out from Werryn, where you work,'
she said. Even further away from my flat than I'd thought.

'Are there trains? Buses?' I asked her.

'Trains, yes. But you're hardly in a fit state to go home by public
transport!'

'My dad will fetch me,' I told her, firmly. I meant Martin of
course. And as I said that I realised it was the night Martin was
going to the Christmas party for his train society. Personally I
imagined it would be about as exciting as watching paint dry but
I know how Martin loves his trains and he has lots of other geek
friends there. I'd feel dead guilty disturbing his big night out. 'Or I
can get a train. I really don't mind. My dad has a party. I don't think
he'll be able to drive.' I couldn't really imagine Martin drunk or
even over the limit, but it didn't seem fair to ruin his night.

'Look, why don't you stay here for the night and we'll sort out
getting you home in the morning?' Christiane's offer took me by
surprise. She really did have a softer side.

'No, I couldn't possibly. I don't want to put you out.'

'You're not putting us out at all. In fact you can keep me
company. The men are going out – some rather dull charity concert
but it's someone that Dermott used to work with. He used to be
a successful conductor before he retired and started hanging
around the house all day, getting under everyone's feet.' Christiane
spoke about her husband like he really irritated her and she
really despised him. It wasn't the nice jokey way Martin and Jane
complained about each other.

So here I am, sitting up in bed and scribbling away, in this dead stylish room, which is coloured all in brown and cream and orange. It ought to be hideous but it kind of works very well, sort of very French and chic. It's warm in here and the bed is soooooo comfy. I even have my own little bathroom off the side of the room. It has a view out over some really high trees.

I can't really believe I'm here – in the house of Tol's parents! The last place in the world I ever wanted to be. But it's not like I've really had to see him at all. After Christiane finished patching me up and she was taking me to the kitchen, I saw him and his dad in penguin suits, looking dead posh and ready to go out to this concert thingy. Tol just smiled and asked me how I was. I was very polite and said I was fine and dead grateful to his mum for looking after me. His mum then announced that I was staying the night and I saw a look of mild panic on his face. It's wrong, but that made me feel good.

After they'd gone I had this really nice meat sauce and rice thing with Christiane, which she said the housekeeper had made. An elderly spaniel arrived and looked at us with big mournful eyes while we ate but Christiane ignored it. 'My husband's dog,' she told me. 'Personally I don't like dogs very much. Animals are a bit of a waste of time in my opinion.'

I stroked the dog under the table when she wasn't looking. It settled on my foot and that felt comforting. It was a bit smelly and shedding hair all over the place, but it was really friendly.

Christiane seemed to relax a bit after a glass of wine. She seemed quite a lot friendlier. She showed me a documentary DVD that a friend of hers had made. It was all about this project in India that's working with kids who sleep on the train station coz they have nowhere else to go. Christiane said she'd been a "consultant" on the programme coz she'd already written a feature about it for one of the Sunday papers. She talked a lot about this guy Jacques who was the producer. She seemed to rate him highly. I did just wonder if... Well, it's not for me to guess about these things but she was a lot nicer about him than her husband or her son. We watched some news after that and I started to feel really sleepy, so Christiane brought me up to this room. She's lent me a nightie and some clean knickers and a toothbrush and stuff. She offered to put my jeans and sweatshirt in the wash but I said I already had spare clothes with me, so it was OK. She wished me a good night and told me to call out if I felt dizzy or needed anything.

I realised after she'd gone that I hadn't brought up a glass of water. I opened my door and hobbled out onto the landing. I could hear a voice, Christiane speaking softly. I suspected she was on the phone, maybe downstairs in that massive dark hall. I caught a few words about 'not home yet' and then the name 'Jacques'. I closed my door and went back to bed. I would make do with water from the sink if I got thirsty.

Oh... just got a text from Dan:

Missin u Hols. Good party. Lots of peeps here. Everyone askin where u r!!!! Lucy turned up with some bloke she sed was her boyf. Thort she wz comin on her own. A bit up hiself. Not like Nathan at all. I liked Nathan. He waz a really nice guy. Sleep well and be careful on that ice!!!

Hmmm. That's not good news. Dan is a good judge of character. Better try to sleep now.

5pm

Tol drove me home! I wasn't going to let him but something he said over breakfast made me decide to.

Christiane told me they normally ate about 8.30am so I was down by then. There was cereal and bagels and bread and stuff left out, and a note from Christiane saying:

Hope you slept well. Had to go into work. Tol will get you home. C

We'll see about that I thought, wondering if there was a local taxi service that could get me to the station. I was just buttering a bagel to take with me and gulping down some coffee with cold water added, when Tol walked in. He said 'Hi' in a sheepish kind of way, and went over to the dog and started fondling its head.

I ignored him and looked around for a cupboard or somewhere I could find some cling film. 'Here,' Tol pulled out a drawer for me. 'There's foil in here. But why don't you sit down and eat. I can drive you home, soon as you're ready. Mum asked me to,' he added, as though this was something he needed to explain.

'And do you do everything your mother asks?' I snapped at him, but quietly.

Tol shrugged. 'No, not all the time, but sometimes it's easier to go along with her. Do you want honey with that? Or peanut butter, or there's cream cheese in the fridge? Or I could cook you some scrambled eggs – we have some smoked salmon.'

I guess he remembered what a good appetite I have and how much I love scrambled egg. He didn't eat that much back then coz of the heroin, but he looks like he eats more these days. He's not quite as skinny as he was – not fat or anything but he's filled out a bit. I think it probably suits him, although I could never fancy him again in a million years.

I heard myself saying OK to the scrambled egg and smoked salmon. It was far better than anything I'd had for brekkie in ages.

'Where does your mum work?' I asked for something to fill the gap, expecting him to say she'd just jumped on a train to London or got a plane to Afghanistan.

'There, just at the bottom of the garden?' Tol pointed to a large shed, about 200 metres from the window.

'Should I go down and thank her for last night?' I asked, wanting an excuse to get out of the kitchen while he cooked.

Ptolemy shook his head firmly. 'No, she won't want that. Nobody disturbs Mum when she's working. It's one of her rules. She asked me to look after you.'

He must have seen the look of slight disappointment on my face. I thought me and Christiane had bonded, just a tiny bit. Now I felt dismissed, put in my place as totally unimportant.

'Hey, don't take it badly,' Tol said, spooning my eggs onto a plate. 'She liked you a lot. She would never have asked you to stay if she didn't. She's just, well, she's just who she is. You get used to her.'

I shrugged, like it meant nothing to me. He sat down opposite me, with a mug of coffee in front of him. I had hoped to enjoy my eggs in peace.

'And thank you Holly. Thank you for not saying anything to her. I really appreciate that.' He said it with a lot of sincerity. It kind of took me by surprise.

'Why would I say anything?' I asked him. 'I'm not a bitch if that's what you're implying.'

'No. I mean, I wasn't implying anything. Just that if I was you I'd have been seriously tempted.'

'Yeah, well, I'm not you,' I said and I started to tuck into my breakfast. I wasn't going to let him spoil it. 'Can I have some more coffee?' I held my mug out to him. I might not be a bitch but that didn't mean I wasn't a manipulative cow.

'How are you feeling today? Are you very sore?' Tol asked as he switched on the kettle. 'And are you going to report that car to the police?'

'Is there any point? I didn't see the car properly.'

'Yeah, but if you're injured and can't work or something... and you might get some compensation. Probably best to report it.'

I laughed out loud. 'You want me to report someone for nearly running me over when you... Well, you know what you did!'

'OK, then this is your opportunity. I run you to the police station and you report both incidents. I will hand myself in. I won't put up any resistance.' Tol raised his hands in a gesture of surrender. I realised then that he really meant it.

'Don't be so bloody stupid,' I told him. 'I have to be back in town pretty soon. But you can give me a lift. It still looks freezing and slippery out there.'

So he drove me home. We didn't really talk coz he asked me to choose a CD and we played that all the way. But it was OK. The journey wasn't as bad as I'd expected. I've heard people say that forgiving people is good for you. I've never quite understood that before, but I could see that Tol was genuinely sorry, so what was the point of me hanging onto my anger? Not everyone can change but maybe some people can. Perhaps a serious shock was what it took for him to change, realising he could have killed someone.

I let him drop me outside the flat. I hadn't meant to do that. I was going to get him to drop me off at the bottom of the road, but my knees were hurting and I admit, I was a bit scared I'd slip again. He wanted to see me to the door and make sure I was OK. I said no, I'd be alright, but I wasn't freaked that he insisted on staying and watching me make my way up the path and to the front door. I trusted that he just wanted to know I got in safely.

After he drove off I realised I hadn't said thank you for driving me home. I felt a bit sorry for that.

I took some painkillers and slept for a bit. Shock can make you feel really strange. I kept feeling like I wanted to cry but I didn't know what I was crying about. I texted Sean to tell him what had happened, thinking he might call me, but I just got a text back saying he was sorry I'd had a fall, and I needed to be careful in the bad weather. I know it's expensive to text Australia and it's probably the middle of the night but...

I need to get my stuff sorted out for housesitting. Hope I manage to spend time with Lucy alone but it doesn't look much like it. I keep getting these texts from her telling me how brilliant Aiden is, and that he wants to take her to X or buy her Y. I think he's full of bull but what would I know?

Mustn't forget to pack you, Diary. Martin is coming to get me in about half an hour. Says he's glad to escape the packing pandemonium going on at home but I think he's worried about me being injured. I really don't hurt as much as I did yesterday. I'm definitely going to live.

TUESDAY 20 DECEMBER

11am - Eating brekkie

I'm sitting in the kitchen at J and M's writing you, Diary. It's freezing outside and I have Boots curled on my lap.

It's calm being in here and calm is what I need coz my head is reeling after what's happened since I left the flat. First of all, there was the phone call from Davina, just as I got out of Martin's car, telling me that Keesh had broken down in tears in the shop and couldn't stop crying. Davina sounded hassled but also kind. She said she'd ordered Keesh a taxi to take her home, told her to take some time off over Christmas and not to worry. She would manage the shop alone for the time being with the part-timer and her partner, Michael. Keesh needed rest she told me; losing her brother had been too much; she'd been working too hard. A flower arrangement had fallen over and splashed a couple of party frocks. It was no disaster but Davina admitted her temper had got the better of her and she'd snapped at Keesh, who'd caught it with her arm. Keesh had snapped back. Davina told me she'd been pretty surprised, coz Keesh was always so in control.

'Maybe I deserved it daahling. I probably did,' Davina told me, sounding genuinely puzzled and concerned. 'But she just went off into the most terrible rant, calling me everything under the sun, blaming me for not understanding her, not trusting her, not having any faith in her. Daahling, I know I'm not the best employer in the world but I don't understand what that was all about.'

I understood because I knew where it was coming from. Like many fostered kids, Keesh had got passed around from one home to the next, always hearing promises about becoming "part of the family", always feeling strange and new and unwanted, and having to fit into somewhere she didn't want to be. Sometimes being with Nathan and sometimes being separated, never really being sure where she'd be at the end of the day, at the end of the week, at the end of the month; turning more and more in on herself for comfort and security, and finding very little inside herself to rely on. And so she created a shell, like most of us do. But for Keesh it was a big, bright, colourful, confident shell. An exotic bird of paradise was my first impression of Keesh and I realised I'd bought into that illusion. I'd actually believed that somehow Keesh was stronger and more together than the rest of us.

'It's not you,' I reassured Davina. 'It's not you she's angry with.'

'I guess it's about her brother,' Davina said.

'Yes, I think it probably is,' I agreed, not wanting to spill any of Keesh's secrets.

'But as soon as she stopped shouting, she just stood there trembling – from head to toe,' Davina continued. 'I think she thought I was going to shout back at her, daahling, sack her on the spot or something. I think some people might have done that...'

Yes, I can imagine lots of employers would have. Not many people give you a second chance. Davina had gone sky high in my estimation.

'I just took her in my arms, held her really tight and she sobbed and sobbed,' Davina explained. 'I told her that I thought she was brave and determined and she was going to be OK. Was that the right thing to do, Holly?'

I couldn't believe that Davina was asking my opinion. 'Definitely the right thing,' I reassured her again. 'Thank you for being so understanding.'

'I know people think I'm hard, selfish even, but I do understand what it's like to be in your position, in Keesh's position.'

I was just wondering what she meant by this when she continued. 'Daahling, I do realise you've both been in care. I was in care for a little while myself. When my mother had her third miscarriage and my father lost his job, my three sisters and I were sent to the local children's home. We absolutely hated it, especially when my youngest sister was separated from us. She was sent to Canada, to be adopted over there, but she died a few months after she arrived. I think she was ill all along and should never have been sent away. It broke our hearts.' I could hear the pain in Davina's voice.

'So daahling, I do understand what it's like to be separated from your parents and to have nobody but your sisters – or in Keesh's case, her brother – to rely on. And losing a sibling is terrible, terrible.'

Davina took a deep breath before carrying on, her tone now totally business-like. Keesh must stay at home and rest till after Christmas. She would be on full pay and her job would remain open for the time being. But she must see her doctor and get some proper help, she must get a sick note and she mustn't think of returning to work until the new year. Davina was trusting me to ensure that all these things happened. And would I promise her I'd take very good care of Keesh over the festive season?

I said, yes, of course I would. I'm not Keesh's mother but if I don't look after her, who will? She doesn't even have Jane and Martin like I do. And she lost contact with her support worker a long time ago.

'And daahling, do try and come to my New Year ball. It's going to be marvellous. And make sure Keesh comes – and bring that delightful friend of yours, the one you showed me the photos of... Lucy isn't it? Such a pretty little thing.'

I promised her I'd do my very best.

I was trying to contact Keesh, when Davina rang back. 'Daahling, this is a bit of an emergency,' she said. 'My part-time lady says she can't possibly do any extra hours and my friend Claudia thinks she's got some hideous sickness bug, and poor dear Michael has man flu. You couldn't possibly work a few days for me over Christmas and New Year could you? Save me having to get in a temp and train them. It wouldn't have to be a full day, just a few hours here and there. You know how I like the shop run and I would pay you very handsomely.'

I wanted to say no, because I had my hours at the garden centre, but the college café was closed in the holidays and... But I also knew that Keesh would fret about her job. And what if she really wasn't well enough to go back? She hadn't been her normal self recently and she might be heading for some major breakdown. Without our two lots of wages coming in there's no way we could afford the rent. The last thing we need is to be homeless. That would be a total disaster. Having our own home is so important to me and Keesh, it's the only space in the world that is truly ours. I think we'd both go crazy shut up in a tiny council flat on some really rough estate where everyone carries knives, and there's dog shit and needles everywhere. There are estates like that by the old canal and I shudder every time I go near them. Too many of the kids I was in care with have ended up in places like that. They have nothing to get up for in the mornings and nobody gives a toss about them. Then people wonder why they get pregnant or drink or get a drug habit or something.

So today I've rung Marje and explained that I have to cut down my hours over Christmas but that Ness is going to do more. I've been in touch with Ness and she's dead pleased about that. Ness needs all the hours she can get to help pay towards uni. I told Marje it's a win-win situation. OK, there maybe won't be any more painted gnomes but then Marje won't have to pay me a bonus, so that will probably suit her as well. And she knows what a brilliant worker Ness is.

Back to last night – I was fretting coz Keesh didn't answer her phone. Then I got a text saying she'd gone to see the minister at her church, so at least she was with someone who would look after her. But I'd told her to get over here asap.

I tried to relax during supper. It was my last big meal with J and M and Ryan and Si before they went to Lapland. Si was too excited to eat coz he knew something was happening but he doesn't really have much grasp of time. Lucy wasn't there because she was out with that Aiden. Again. So Ruby was sitting in her high chair and happily making a right old mess with the sticky chocolate pud that Martin had baked for a special treat. Ryan was quiet but he seemed to be eating, and I didn't want to risk winding him up in any way. But every time I looked at him I thought about that bloody scratch on his arm. Were there other ones? And were they deeper or just the same? And were there other marks on other parts of his body? How long had he been doing this and just how serious was it? It scared me to think my little brother was cutting himself with that horrible sharp blade I'd seen. But most of all it scared me that he might do something really serious with that knife... I knew then that I had to tell Martin or Jane before they went. I couldn't risk leaving it.

'Is everyone packed?' Martin said suddenly. 'And how many thermal vests is too many? Should I take four pairs of gloves? Or five?'

Ryan shot my foster father that look of contempt he gives any adult (me included) who tries to make a vaguely humorous comment these days. But Si looked up from the mashed potato he was pushing around his plate. 'Dinosaurs,' he said.

'And just how many dinosaurs are you taking?' Martin asked him. (Jane had already explained to me that they'd had to persuade Si not to take his entire model collection.)

Si looked very thoughtful for a moment and then carefully held up eight fingers.

'Oh Lord,' Jane said, 'I thought we'd agreed no more than five, young man?'

Si met her eye for a moment. He did a little shrug and then slowly, one by one, curled up the fingers on his right hand.

'Five dinosaurs,' Martin counted. 'No, wait a minute... four dinosaurs. I see a thumb going down there.'

Si nodded. 'Four,' he said, very quietly. 'Big ones.'

Jane burst out laughing, and Martin and I joined in. Ruby just giggled and waved her spoon coz everyone else was laughing. Even Ryan managed a bit of a grin and Simon looked enormously pleased with himself.

'Are you packed yet?' I asked Jane, when we were bathing Ruby, while the men did the washing up.

'You must be joking,' Jane replied. 'I'll be shovelling my stuff in tonight.'

'I guess packing for the boys takes time,' I said.

'Oh, they're no problem,' Jane told me. 'But Martin is a nightmare. He's packed and unpacked his stuff about 47 times. I've had to get quite strict with him!'

'She won't let me take my Santa pyjamas,' Martin informed me, sticking his head through the open bathroom door.

'That's because you're already taking the Rudolph pyjamas which are much warmer. How many sets of pyjamas does a man need for a three-night stay?'

Christmas pyjamas are a tradition in this house. J and M's son Leon always sends his dad a new pair over from Canada each year.

'Eight,' Martin said, holding up the required number of fingers. 'Or maybe just four, especially if they are large ones.'

Ruby splashed water into my eyes at that moment, otherwise I'd probably have been snorting with laughter like Jane.

After that I didn't really want to spoil the cosy atmosphere. Also it didn't seem right to talk about my brother cutting himself, in front of Ruby. You can never tell how much little kids understand and Ruby has this way of repeating words without knowing what they mean. But then after bathtime, it was really difficult getting Jane or Martin on their own. Ryan hung around till way past his normal bedtime and Jane didn't seem to notice coz she was all over the house hunting out all the last-minute bits and pieces, and writing notes and generally being terribly organised and crazily busy. But I knew she'd have to go upstairs soon to do her own packing so I made some excuse about being tired and needing to go to bed. I went to give my brother a hug but he just sat stiffly watching the TV. I noticed him looking down at the cuts on my hands where I'd pulled the plasters off coz they kept getting wet. I realised that he'd probably forgotten about my accident, or maybe he just didn't register it because there was so much else on his mind.

Martin wasn't exactly available either. Si couldn't settle coz he'd got all worked up. J and M had been talking to him about the holiday for days and explaining over and over again what was happening to try and keep him from getting too stressed, but there's so much stuff going on in Si's head that you never know what he registers and what he forgets. It's like nobody really knows what he feels about the night that his uncle killed Nathan or what exactly he remembers about the stabbing.

I was all ready to pounce on Jane as she went into her bedroom to pack her own suitcase but then my phone rang and it was Keesh. She told me she was feeling a bit better but she was going to stay over with the minister and her family for the night. But she agrees she's going to come over here tomorrow, to stay with me at J and M's. She sounds dead embarrassed. Poor Keesh, she's so used to being in control of everything.

By the time I was free again I could hear Jane downstairs, talking firmly to my brother and telling him he had to go to bed. I thought it wouldn't be long before she came upstairs again so I decided to have a little nap.

When I woke up with all my clothes on it was the middle of the night and all the lights were out. There was gentle snoring coming from J and M's room. So I got up and wrote a note:

Dont want you to worry but I think it important you know that Ryan is cutting himself with a knife. I think its what they call self harm and I think you know about this from your training. Please keep a good eye on him while you away.

PS I was going to tell you to your faces but I didnt get the chance

PPS Have a great holiday and dont worry

I slid the note under J and M's door so they would find it when they woke up.

The taxi came at 7.30am and I got up to see them off. There was no sign of Lucy but I opened her front door and called up the stairs. She appeared a few minutes later, looking flustered. I got the feeling she wasn't alone up there. Or maybe she was embarrassed that I was holding her daughter. Jane had taken Ruby into her bedroom when it was clear that Lucy was staying out late, and I'd found her juggling a grisly toddler while she tried to supervise the boys' breakfast, and Martin was outside loading the car. So I'd taken Ruby myself. Luce held out her arms the minute she saw her daughter but I wasn't impressed. 'Your mum had loads to do, she didn't need to be worrying about your daughter too,' I hissed at her. 'You ought to apologise.'

Lucy glared back at me. 'Mum likes having Ruby. She told me so.'

'Yeah, but maybe not when she's trying to pack her suitcase and organise the boys for an early start,' I replied.

Lucy stuck out her bottom lip but that killer pout only works on blokes. I wasn't impressed. I was too busy worrying about my brother to fret about her.

I tried not to make a big thing of saying goodbye to Ryan. I hugged J and M and I solemnly shook Si's hand. I wanted to hug my brother but I thought he'd freak out, so I kind of crept up behind him as he was walking out the door and gave him a quick back-to-front hug, planting a kiss on his head.

'Stop it,' he said, predictably shrugging me off, but I got the feeling he didn't really mind.

The minute the waving off was finished, Lucy turned on her heels and stomped off upstairs. I called after her, 'Hey wait, Lucy, come and have a cuppa with me in the kitchen.' After all we were going to spend the next four days under the same roof, even if she has her own flatlet bit. And she is my BF. I didn't want us to be mad at each other.

My foster sister just carried on, with a sleepy Ruby peering at me over her shoulder. 'I've got my own kitchen,' Lucy told me, her sharp tone drifting down from the top of the stairs. 'Anyway, I want to go back to bed...'

I took a deep breath. 'Look, Luce, I'm just here because your mum and dad worry about you being alone after what happened. I know you don't need me to look after you.'

'Funny that,' Lucy said, turning briefly to look down at me. 'Coz I seem to remember you were the one who was here when... when it happened...'

'So why don't you come down and keep me company? There's that spare bed in our old room. You could come and join me.'

But Lucy wasn't listening. She was opening up her little dividing door, the one that separated her living space from the rest of the house.

As I went past J and M's room I glanced in, checking to see what kind of mess they'd left it in. The first thing I noticed was this little bit of whiteness sticking out from *under* the frayed edges of the carpet. There was my note completely unnoticed and unread. I felt sick with despair and wanted to cry.

As I was standing there, I felt something soft against my ankle. Boots was rubbing himself furiously against my legs. I suspected he'd already had breakfast when Martin got up, but he was clearly after a second one. So here we are, me and Boots having breakfast together, watching a few swirls of snow trying to settle but melting on contact with the ground.

I could sit here all day, Diary, but I guess I'd better go and get myself dressed. Perhaps I'll just have one more coffee before I do...

Midnight

Here I am again, waiting for Lucy to get in. Feels like Lucy and that boyf of hers have become the focus of my day. Hmmm.

I was making that second coffee in the kitchen this morning, when I heard footsteps on the stairs. Thinking it was Lucy I put my nose out of the kitchen door to say hi. Coming down the stairs was someone completely different.

'Morning, Aiden,' I said, brightly.

He glanced up from studying the stair carpet and mumbled something that could have been 'mornin' or might have been 'drop dead'. He's not what you'd call a happy, friendly chappy. He kept walking out through the hall, almost slamming the front door behind him. Some people just aren't morning people.

I checked my email today to see if there's been any reply from my dad. What I found made me feel sick with rage. That rottweiler secretary had written that Mr Richards had asked her to say that he didn't know the people concerned and while he was sorry to hear about someone who was so ill, he really didn't see how he could help. He felt I must have mistaken him for someone else.

Yeah, very likely.

There was also a message from Sean to say he hoped I was looking after myself. That he loves me and misses me, and wishes he was here to kiss my cuts better. Aww, that is rather sweet.

I was working on my dress for Davina's NY eve ball when Keesh's minister dropped her off. She seemed nice, and very modern and open minded. Not fuddy duddy and set in her ways like some of the vicars and pastors I remember, coz some of my foster carers were dead religious and used to make me go to church with them. She stopped for a quick cuppa with us. She told me stories about some of the weird situations she's found herself in as a minister – like the woman whose huge boobs fell out of her low-cut dress as she knelt down to pray, and how she had to cover up a fit of the giggles by pretending to have a coughing fit, coz the woman hadn't noticed and the man kneeling next to her nearly died of embarrassment – and that really made me laugh.

Keesh got out some sewing of her own and the two of us sat quietly for a bit, both working on some fiddly hand-stitching stuff and half watching a really bad Christmas comedy on the TV. After a while I said, 'How you doing?' and Keesh said 'Fine'. But then she started to cry, big sobs shaking her shoulders and tears pouring down her cheeks. I wanted to let it all come out, so I didn't hug her, just knelt beside her, holding her hand and making soothing noises.

'I so scared,' Keesh blurted out, eventually. 'I so scared I gonna lose my mind... my job, our flat... then I become some crazy lady in a mental ward and...'

Keesh stopped suddenly, embarrassed. 'Hey,' she said. 'Hey, I'm cryin' here and you is worrying 'bout your mum. I not even asked you how she's doin'.'

I realised that I hadn't thought about Mum for hours. I'd been so busy thinking about Ryan and Lucy and Keesh, and everyone else I needed to worry about.

I got Keesh to make an appointment with her GP. I had to take the phone away from her and tell the receptionist that 'No, it can't wait till after Christmas' and that she needed to be seen urgently. I told the receptionist that my friend was cracking up and her employer said she had to see the doctor urgently. The receptionist said if she was that bad then maybe I ought to take her to A&E. I told her that Keesh needed to see her own GP. I explained that her brother had been murdered recently and she needed to see someone she knew. The receptionist said that maybe I should contact the community psychiatric team. I said that people usually need a referral to the team and the doctor was the best person to do this. (I know these things coz of my brother. And Mum.)

So they squeezed Keesh in somehow and we went together to see the doc at 4.45. The snow was quite deep so I used some of the emergency money J and M left to get a taxi. I hope they won't mind. Keesh didn't need me to go in with her coz she's a big girl, and I read some grubby old mags in the waiting room. Funny all that stuff about hand gel and then they have disgusting mags lying around. Don't know why I read them but there was this article about a woman who claimed her husband was a cannibal and ate three of her neighbours. And you gotta read stuff like that, haven't you ☺?

Keesh came out of the appointment looking happier. The doctor said it was probably delayed stress and grief and a whole load of pressure to keep going when maybe she should have taken it a bit easier. She's got a prescription for some tablets to help her relax and a sick note for work. She has to take things easy and go back again after Christmas for a follow-up. And she can have some free counselling, if she's happy to go on a waiting list.

'Sheesh, girl,' Keesh said, popping the first tablet when we got home. 'Can't kinda believe this is happenin' to me!'

I got her to talk about how she was feeling and she said she was worried about her job. She knows she's lucky to have someone as understanding as Davina for a boss, but she realises Davina won't keep her job open for ever. And benefits probably wouldn't cover her share of the rent.

'But you'll always get work,' I reassured her. 'You've always done. You've waitressed and worked in cafés and nightclubs. You could blag your way into anywhere!'

But Keesh just sighed and said she didn't feel that confident any more. The thought of walking in somewhere and demanding a job made her feel panicky. She told me that she'd had nightmares about ending up alone and homeless, one of those people who sit in doorways and beg for coins from passers by.

'I was never goin' there girl. I was goin' to be someone who made good. Who never fulfilled no stereotypes... And look at me, girl, cryin' like a baby and takin' these pills...'

I put my arms round her and told her that she had already "made good". I told her that many people would have fallen apart totally if their brother had been murdered, especially when he was the main person in their life. It was coz she was so strong that she'd held up for so long.

'Sure hun, I know, but I has no one there for me. You have Jane and Martin and Lucy an' Ryan. Me and Nathe fought a lot but he was all I had.' She told me, not resentfully or anything but just stating it how it is.

I reminded her that we care leavers have to look after each other, that we're like family, that I was going to be there for her, whatever happened. And I most certainly wouldn't let her end up homeless.

'Bless you, babe, I don' want to be a burden to you. You has your own problems.'

I told her that she's never a burden. She's been there for me in the past and I know she'll be there for me in the future.

But I'll tell you who is being a bit of a burden at the moment and that's Lucy. She and Keesh could be such a support to each other, coz they have so much in common. Besides we're all here under the same roof. But Lucy just breezes down about 7pm, all chatty and giggly and says hi to Keesh like she hasn't noticed Keesh is all puffy, red-eyed and fragile. The old Lucy was the kindest person I knew. Who took her away and sent this self-centred girl back in her place?

Lucy says she hopes we don't mind but she's got a party to go to, and would we look after Ruby for her. I was all ready to say no coz I think this going out all the time is too much, but Keesh said yes, she'd love to look after little Ruby. She was actually smiling as she said it, so I didn't have the heart to contradict her. OK, I thought, but just this one night.

So me and Keesh spent the evening in watching crappy films and eating mince pies with ice cream. Jane left sooooo much food in the fridge and she told me and Lucy we had to eat lots of it coz there'd never be any room for the turkey if we didn't. So what else can you do?

That Aiden came and picked Lucy up. I like him less and less. He stood around scowling in the downstairs hallway while Lucy was bringing down last-minute things that me and Keesh needed to look after Ruby. I could hear him tapping his foot and swearing under his breath. I should have been polite and asked him to wait with us in the sitting room but I didn't want to.

Lucy was all flustered when she left. She bundled Ruby into my arms and dropped the last of her daughter's toys onto the floor. 'It's OK Lucy,' I said, as she pecked me quickly on the cheek. 'You don't need to worry. We can always get anything you've forgotten. You'll leave the flat door unlocked won't you?'

'You shouldn't need anything,' Lucy said quickly, pulling away from me and going across to give Keesh a quick little hug before kissing her daughter one more time.

Mr Terribly Pleased with Himself Aiden roared away in his car. 'Wonder what he got for his birthday?' Keesh grinned at me. 'What she doin' with a plonker like him?'

'You tell me,' I shrugged at Keesh, as we both started trying to distract Ruby with her toys. She had held out her plump little arms and run to follow Lucy as she disappeared out of the door. Keesh caught her up in her arms and she'd whimpered 'Mummy' in a voice that hurt my heart.

'Hush precious girl... yo' Auntie Keesh is here for you.'

It was OK: me and Keesh and Ruby. It was like being at home but away from home. 'Maybe we need to go and check on the flat tomorrow,' I told Keesh. 'Make sure none of the pipes are freezing.'

Then Keesh got a phone call from her minister and she went into the kitchen to answer it. I bundled up Ruby in all her warmest clothes and we went out and checked the bunnies' water wasn't frozen. Ruby was fascinated, as ever, by watching the two rabbits watching us and had a great big smile on her face. I put an extra layer of sacking over the hutch. They looked snug with all that extra hay and straw I've put in for them, but rabbits can die if it gets too cold. They're two sisters called Poppy and Hoppy; at least they have each other to snuggle up to. I wished I had Sean tonight but he's in this amazing beach house on a place called Moreton Island, where there are dolphins and giant crabs and wallabies and giant turtles. It does sound like heaven. His aunt and uncle live in Brisbane but they've got this little holiday place they rent from friends and they're spending Christmas there. OK for some!

Keesh came back looking a bit awkward. 'The minister ask if I want to go on this retreat thing. They had it planned for a likkle while... some of them going to this monastery for a few days to prepare for Christmas. Get a bit of a spiritual focus an' get away from all the shoppin' and commercial stuff... I couldn't go coz of work and money and stuff, but someone got flu and there's this spare place. All paid for.'

My heart sank. Just when I felt I was getting cosy here with Keesh. But I tried not to look disappointed.

'A retreat?' I asked, brightly. 'Isn't that a lot of praying and silence and... ?

'Yeah, meditation and stuff, and time fo' talkin' and reflectin' and just bein' quiet. The monks are dead nice apparently and do amazin' food... '

'Probably exactly what you could do with right now,' I heard myself saying, while inside I'm thinking, 'Don't go Keesh, don't leave me alone in this house with Crazy Lucy...'

So it's all fixed. The minister will be collecting Keesh tomorrow morning and driving her down to Wales, where they'll be staying in a fabulous old castle, run by a lot of jolly monks who, according to the website, 'welcome people from all faiths to come and refresh their souls'. It's not my scene, but it does sound peaceful and the photos make it look very beautiful. I think the break will be just what Keesh needs right now. And afterwards the minister has asked Keesh to stay with her and her family for the Christmas weekend to help them serve the meal for homeless people, and other things the church has planned. I wondered how Keesh would feel about that but she said that felt good too. 'It's like what you said, girl,' she told me. 'We care leavers got to stick together. Some of the homeless people we gonna be lookin' after, they grew up in care.'

Keesh has gone up to bed coz she needs an early night, but I'm down here sitting by the gas fire with Boots on my lap and Ruby asleep in her cot. And it's just you and me, Diary. I wonder when that maddening girl Lucy is coming home. Jane texted to say they'd arrived safely and the hotel was comfortable even if it's a bit over the top with cheesy Christmas stuff, and to ask if everything was OK. I said yes, fine. I don't want her worrying about things this end.

Jane said that the journey went OK and the boys were pretty chilled on the flight. That was good to hear. I thought about saying something about Ryan cutting, but I couldn't think of the best way to do it by text. Anyway Jane isn't the most technical person and I worried that Ryan might see the message somehow. He'd feel so betrayed that I'd broken my promise. It could push him to do something crazy, I know what my brother is like. So I just said: *Please take good care of my brother* and then I added: *Which I know u always do* ☺.

WEDNESDAY 21 DECEMBER

I was nearly late for work at the boutique. But that was because I had a major row with Lucy at 4am this morning. I'd nodded off by the fire waiting for her to come in, and woke up to hear Lucy giggling like a naughty schoolchild as she stumbled on the stairs, with Aiden stomping on her heels.

My back and neck had got stiff in the chair and I wasn't in the best of moods.

'What the f*** are you doing?' I demanded, flicking all the lights on in the hall. 'Trying to sneak in like that when I've been sitting up with your daughter all night?'

Two faces turned to look at me. One pink and flushed and guilty. One cold and irritated.

'Oh Hols, so sorreee. We dijunt mean to wake 'shoo… ' Lucy was slurring her words. I could tell she was very drunk.

'Yeah, well that's hardly the point. What about your daughter?' I was dead livid that Lucy seemed to have forgotten all about her child.

'Hey, lady – I don't know what your problem is but you back off!' Aiden turned on me with a really menacing expression.

I had to restrain myself from slapping him. How dare he speak to me like that in my foster carers' house?

'Soweee Hols, we went to this h...' but Lucy couldn't finish her sentence, and stopped to burp loudly. 'Oooops... think thosh pina coladas are...' and at that point she was very sick on the stairs.

Aiden just stormed off and I heard a click and then the door slamming to Lucy's flat. (Oh no, stupid girl, she's gone and given him a key!) Meanwhile Lucy lay down on the top of the landing and fell fast asleep. So guess who spent the next 20 minutes going up and down the stairs with bin bags and cleaning cloths and cleaning foam and air freshener? Yeah, you guessed right. And guess who then shook and dragged a floppy and whingeing Lucy into Si's bedroom coz it was the nearest to the stairs and Lucy's not a small girl? Yeah, right again.

She smelt vile coz she'd thrown up all down herself and the vomit was in her hair, her clothes and on her hands. I tried to get her out of some of her clothes and give her a bit of a wipe with a towel. I fetched a t-shirt from my suitcase to dress her in. I think she'd probably wee'd herself as well but I wasn't checking that far down. I made Lucy as comfortable as I could and put a bucket beside the bed, and some towels around her. She was snoring loudly by the time I'd done all that.

Then I went down to fetch Ruby who was also still fast asleep. Some time around 5am I nodded off with her close by my bed. At about quarter to six Ruby woke me up, whimpering for her mummy. I gave her a big cuddle and some of those rusk biscuit things she loves. Keesh turned in her sleep and mumbled something about helping but I told her to stay where she was. She needs all the rest her poor head can get. Ruby cheered up a bit but was all wide awake so I played with her for a while. I even checked to see if her mum was in any fit state to care for her, but she was lying on her back, snorting and snuffling like a dragon. I wondered about taking

Ruby into the bed with me but I remembered all that stuff Lucy had said about the number of small children who get suffocated when an adult rolls on them in their sleep. Bloody hell! I feel so responsible for everything and everybody. It really isn't fair.

I was down in the kitchen making Ruby's porridge and putting out cat bowls when that Aiden came stomping down the stairs and slammed the front door. 'Stay away from my sister!' I yelled at his back. For all the good it did me.

I woke Keesh up before I left, to hand Ruby over to her and say goodbye. She was making a big effort to be bright and breezy and I think the retreat is going to be good for her. I made her promise to text me a lot while she's away. I also made her give me the minister's number and I told her she had to give the minister my number too. Just in case. OMG, I'm so organised sometimes, I feel like I'm a hundred. Need someone to rewind and get me back to being 19!

Keesh gave me a Christmas card to give to Davina. She said there was a little letter in there thanking her for being so kind. I said I thought that was really nice, and I'd tell Davina that she is doing everything she can to make a quick recovery.

'Oh Lord, a retreat!' Davina cried, shrilling with laughter. 'You young people, you never cease to surprise me. I'd have been home taking drugs and listening to psychedelic music, and crying into my pillow. Goodness, daahling, your generation is so much more practical and resourceful. At least she will get plenty of rest there. I think it's lights out by 9 o'clock and no talking in these religious places. Awfully good for the complexion – and the nerves.'

I'd told Davina about the GP appointment and handed over the sick note and she was touched by Keesh's card. 'She's a dear girl,' Davina told me, 'I do miss her. But it's splendid to have you here daahling. Now shall we take a look at the knitwear section? I had two customers in here yesterday who absolutely devastated it. It's like a battlefield!'

The day went by quite fast. I've done odd days in the boutique before so I kind of know the routine. The golden rule is to be very nice to customers at all times, show them whatever they ask to see and offer them a cup of tea or glass of mineral water if they want to sit down, or a glass of champagne if they have loads and loads of money to spend.

Lots of customers came into the shop. People were looking for last-minute Christmas and New Year outfits and the wealthy ones were looking for presents for family and friends. I ended up modelling a beautiful zebra-print skirt and rollneck jumper in the fluffiest, softest angora for a very large, orange-tanned woman who was buying for her "model" daughter.

'Ah, my Leila would look beautiful in that,' the woman said, patting me on the cheek with an immaculately manicured hand as she left the shop clutching a couple of bulging carrier bags. 'Thank you dearie, for showing me how stunning it can be.'

When the customer was safely out of earshot Davina couldn't wait to tell me: 'The daughter, Leila, has had more facelifts than I've had hot dinners. And breast implants and tummy tucks, and lord only knows what else – hard to imagine what she hasn't had, daahling! Such a pity. She won't look a fraction as good as you do in that adorable little twinset. I do like my clothes to go to good homes.'

Davina took a sip of the champagne she'd poured herself. She always has one if it's been opened for the customers, but never any more. She'd offered me a glass but I'd said no. I thought I might fall over if I had alcohol on top of all that tiredness.

'Anyway daahling, according to my hairdresser, Leila is currently married to that horribly ugly footballer. You know which one I mean... always in the papers for shagging call girls and behaving like a thug. Of course daahling, I have no interest in any of them, but it's important to keep up with a bit of the gossip, don't you think?' Davina had a very naughty twinkle in her eye.

It was supper time before I got to look at my messages. Keesh had texted to say that Lucy had finally got up and taken over the care of her daughter. Keesh said she seemed very quiet and guilty for what had happened, and she'd apologised for being sick.

I found a message from Lucy saying exactly that, but no mention of an apology for leaving us to care for her daughter. Or for having such an idiot for a boyfriend. I would be having strong words later.

But when I got home Lucy wasn't there. There was a note saying:

Hey Holly – thanx a million for last night. Must have been something I ate! Ruby is next door, with Mrs Stoker. I wont be back for a bit coz Ade is taking me to some fab party down in the West End of London with celebs and some of his model friends... I will make it up to you soon, Hols. I promiz. Big hugs Lucy

'She said it was a bit of an emergency – and that you'd be back soon,' Mrs Stoker explained anxiously. She's quite a frail old lady and I don't think she was very happy being left to care for a small child. I wasn't happy either, so I knew where she was coming from. I apologised and told her it wouldn't happen again.

'You're such a good girl,' Mrs Stoker told me, as I left. 'Come and see me over Christmas. I get lonely.' (I know that's not true coz she's always invited to J and M's if she's on her own and she never comes.)

I sent Lucy a very angry text and I left her a furious message on her phone. I said it wasn't fair – I'd been working all day and I had to be at the garden centre tomorrow. She had nothing to do but sit on her fat butt and go partying. She needed to come home and care for her own child.

Lucy hasn't answered any of my messages. I've tried her again several times. I am quite worried about her but I'm also pretty sure she'll be with that Aiden. He's an idiot but I don't think he's a rapist or a murderer. Oh bloody hell, I hope not! No point me ringing the police coz they won't be interested. She's 18 and she's out with a boy from free choice. It's not like she's been kidnapped.

In the last message I left Lucy I did a mean thing. I kind of hinted I was thinking of calling social services and telling them to come and fetch Ruby if she didn't come home straight away. But she knows I won't. She knows that it's something I'd never do coz I know how it would affect Ruby. At least Ruby knows me and she knows this house. It's different to going to some strange foster carer's home. And just think of the shame for poor J and M – the grand-daughter of well-known foster carers taken into care when they're out of the country for 10 minutes! I couldn't do that to them.

But how am I going to manage with a toddler to look after and a job to go to? I can't let Marje down. She'll decide I'm dead unreliable and I – well, me and Keesh – need my salary more than ever.

Sean texted me tonight to say he misses me something rotten. I wish he was here. What use is he to me on the other side of the world? I tried Dan but he's got work himself tomorrow. He was sounding pretty cut up himself. He said he'd finished with Rani because he just knew she was getting ready to dump him. When he told her she'd said that it was "probably for the best". Dan thinks that maybe she was introduced to someone at her cousin's wedding, someone that her parents want her to marry. He said he hoped she was doing this because she really likes this person, not coz her family have pressurised her. But he also said it's not his problem. He's tried so hard to make things work with her and he realises now that she was probably never going to settle down with him.

I feel awful for him but I can't really cope with anyone else's stuff just now. But Dan said that he was fine. He's a bloke and blokes are crap at "handling feelings", so he'll probably go out and drink too much with his mates and he'll have a bloody good cry when he's drunk enough. I told him that I thought that was a terrible idea and reminded him that he could call me any time he needed to talk. And I asked him if he had the number for the Samaritans and he laughed and said that Rani isn't worth killing himself for, and that made me feel a bit better. But then I started thinking about my brother and my stomach hurt with the stress of everything and I wanted to give Ruby a cuddle, but that just made her cry.

I put her down in her playpen and she settled with some chunky farmyard toys which she was trying to force inside a teapot from her pretend tea set and they wouldn't fit coz they were too wide. But that didn't bother her and she went on trying to shove them in. She has a lot of determination that child... perhaps a little bit of stubbornness. Maybe she takes after me ☺.

I just couldn't think who else I'd trust to look after a young toddler. What a nightmare! Keesh, Lucy, Sean, Jane and Martin, the people I normally trust more than anyone else, none of them any good at the moment. And they've kind of caused this situation in the first place. Well, no, that's not fair. The blame lies squarely at Lucy's door; she's the one who's done a runner and left me with her daughter to look after. The rest just happen to not be available.

I was hunting through my handbag to see if I could find the number for a girl from college to see if she still does babysitting, when a piece of paper fell out: Ptolemy's phone number.

'You'd trust me with a small child?' he asked, totally surprised after he'd got over the shock that I'd phoned him in the first place.

'Well, no, I wouldn't... no... but you take me and her to the garden centre and you stay with her there. It's warm in the coffee shop and I can also ask my boss if we can use her office, so I can check her every time I get a break. You may be an idiot but I don't suspect you of being a child abuser!'

'OK, I get it,' Ptolemy said, 'I'll see if I can change my plans for tomorrow.'

'There's no "see" about it,' I told him. 'You said you wanted to apologise in some way, and this is the way you can start doing it...'

So it's fixed. Ptolemy is coming here at 7.45am and me and Ruby will be ready for him. I know it's not an ideal situation, giving this guy who nearly killed my brother my precious god-daughter to mind. Everything I know about child protection stuff says this isn't a good idea. But my gut instinct tells me that he would never deliberately harm anybody. I do believe that he didn't actually give my brother the drugs. Ryan admits he probably helped himself when Tol was passed out. I think Tol has turned over a new leaf. He does seem different – more responsible and mature. It's a less than perfect solution but I can only do the best I can do, and I will be checking Ruby every half an hour or so.

Now I need to sleep. I'm so wired up that I can't seem to rest.

Oh, there's one other thing. I got another reply from that stupid secretary woman of my dad's. She's getting really snippy with me, telling me she will get emails from me barred if I continue to hassle Mr Richards. Charming. Since when has two messages been "hassling"?

THURSDAY 22 DECEMBER

Writing this in front of the TV. It's been a long day and I need an early night.

Ruby woke me up crying again, but I didn't really mind. I was having another nightmare about Ryan. And Nathan. It was that summer all over again and Si's vile relatives were here trying to kidnap him. Only this time, after poor Nathan was stabbed, Ryan didn't chase after the killers. He rushed at the man who was holding the knife and grabbed it from him. I knew what my brother was going to do with the knife but I didn't know how to stop him. I heard him whimpering with pain and there was blood everywhere and it was dripping down the stairs...

But it wasn't Ryan whimpering; it was poor Ruby who was sobbing, 'Mummy, Mummy', and also needed her nappy changing. I was so tired that as soon as she was settled again I was back to sleep, with the alarm set for 6.45am.

There was no sign of Lucy when I got up, so there was no choice. Ruby was coming to work with me.

People at the garden centre were dead nice about having her there. I explained that she's my best friend's baby and I'd had to bring her with me, coz of "personal stuff", and I'd brought a "minder" as well so it wouldn't interfere with my work. Marje and Rhonda went all gooey at the sight of a cute toddler and I have to say Tol's big green eyes had their normal effect. Marje insisted that he could sit in her office where it was cosy for Ruby, and Rhonda kept popping in every five mins to check that they were doing OK. Even the Christmas tree boy went all soppy when he saw Ruby and started making silly baby talk. It made my life much easier knowing that so many people were looking out for that little girl. Pity her mother wasn't one of them! I just don't understand it. Lucy was such a devoted mum and then she meets some boy who gives her a bit of attention and she drops everything to run after him.

Ness came in this afternoon. She was doing a late-night shift but she'd come in a bit early to catch me. It's the first time I've actually set eyes on her since she's come back from college. It was brilliant to see her and I think I probably shed a tear or two when she asked how I was doing. Then she insisted I told her what was going on and while I painted a gnome in a stripy business suit, I confided in her what's been happening with Lucy. She said I could have called her last night, which I hadn't thought about. 'But that Tol seems a really nice guy,' she said. 'He's very gentle with little Ruby.' And I had to remind myself that she hadn't *really* been there that day when Tol had reappeared in my life.

'Ah,' I said, 'there's a history behind him. He's not always been such a saint.'

'Have any of us?' Ness asked.

'C'mon, Ness ... this guy used to have a really bad heroin habit. He swears he's totally clean now and it was a couple of years ago, but I'm not sure I should be letting him look after a child.'

Ness didn't look as shocked as I'd expected. 'My girlfriend Bea had a bit of a shady past,' Ness admitted, quietly, coz Duane was hanging around in the background, trying to sneak a peek at me.

'Look, I know Bea wouldn't mind me sharing this coz she's not ashamed of her past, and she still works with people in recovery as a volunteer. She had a really tough childhood and ran away from home... got into prostitution to feed her drug habit. Then she met some people from a brilliant outreach project. They helped her make a fresh start, go to college, think about who she was and what she wanted to become, which is how she got into garden design. I find it hard to picture her having a habit or street walking because that was about five years ago, before I met her, and these days she's such a together kind of person. It shows that people can change, if they really want to.'

Well, would you believe it! I knew Bea was about four years older than Ness but I'd somehow imagined her as this quiet, gentle soul, a bit intense and very serious about everything, without a wild bone in her body. A bit like Ness herself. Just shows you never can tell.

'OK,' I said. 'The evidence so far suggests that Ptolemy is really making an effort to stay clean and feels bad about what happened. He has been trying to be really nice to me, and very gentle with Ruby. He turned up this morning with bagels and cream cheese and smoked salmon, and the most divine hot chocolate. And he played with Ruby and fed the rabbits, cleared up a hairball from the cat and stacked the dishwasher. He spent ages fitting the baby seat just right in the car, and he drove dead carefully on the icy roads.'

'So what about Sean?' Ness asked.

'What about Sean?'

'Are you still together?'

'Yes, of course. Very much so. It's just that I'm a teeny bit pissed off with him at the moment.'

'Yes, I got that from your texts.'

'It's his mother. She always has to be the centre of everything and I can't believe how he runs around after her. My mum is really dying but his mum's got some little lump that will probably turn out to be nothing.' I couldn't say any more because I could feel the tears threatening again.

'Come here, Hols, you need a hug. You're completely exhausted,' Ness folded me against her neat little body, patting me on the back like I was a baby needing burping.

The trouble with me is that once someone is really nice to me I can't stop crying. Ness had to take me into a quiet corner of the storeroom where I snivelled my eyes out. I told her about Mum and Keesh and disappearing Lucy, and how I was worried sick about my brother.

'You've just got too much on your plate. It isn't fair on you,' Ness said, offering me yet another tissue. 'So what are we going to do to sort it out?'

'There's nothing anyone can do,' I told Ness. 'But it's only for a few days. Martin and Jane will be home by Christmas Eve. I just have to hang on until they get back.'

'But can you manage to hold on till then? You do have to think about yourself. You're only 19, Holly. You shouldn't have to run everyone else's lives for them.'

'But somebody has to,' I wept into Ness's shoulder. 'Somebody has to be in control.'

'No, no they don't,' Ness told me gently. 'People have to take responsibility for themselves and you worrying yourself sick isn't helping anyone.'

I caught sight of the clock on the wall. Time was running away with itself. 'Oh Lord, I haven't checked on Ruby for ages... and Marje will be wondering where we are...'

'Ruby is fine. When I went past Marje's office she had her sitting on her lap, while she was doing some stuff on the computer. Well, trying to. You know how hopeless Marje is, and your Ptolemy was sitting beside her and showing her how to do various things to make it easier. I'm sure I heard the term "defragging" being used.'

Ness took me by the shoulders and gently pushed me away from her. 'Now let's just think about all of this. Your friend Keesh is fine, she's with a lot of religious types who will look after her, so she's not your responsibility. If she can't return to work you may have to give up your flat, but that isn't the end of the world. People do survive in council flats, honestly they do. My mum lives in quite a nice one, where I grew up.'

Funny, I'd had this impression of Ness growing up in some posh old house. Maybe not a big one but... Her mum is really clever, teaches evening classes and has thousands of books, according to Ness. I'd never pictured her living on a council estate.

'And your brother is with Jane and Martin, who must have cared for plenty of kids who self-harm. He couldn't be in a safer place. I bet he's probably having a really good time.'

Well, Jane had texted this morning that both the boys did seem to be enjoying themselves. Maybe a total change of scene was doing my brother good, but what about when he came back?

'That's then and this is now,' Ness told me firmly. 'Holly Richards, has nobody ever told you that worrying about something doesn't make it any better? But you have to tell Jane and Martin about him cutting himself. Why don't you text or ring them if you're so worried?'

'But he said he'd "do something" if someone found out. I have to be really careful. My brother likes to make a point. I'm dead scared he might try and run away out there and...'

'Then you need to text Jane and Martin and say that you need to speak to them in private, that it's nothing to worry about but you need some advice. You don't have to say what it's about. You're always saying that they're such brilliant foster carers. I really think you should trust them.'

'OK,' I said, 'I'll think about that.' She was right of course.

'Please do. And as for your mum, Hol, that's just horrible and you have a right to be really sad. But is there anything you can actually do? You've tried your dad and it hasn't worked. What do you need to do for you? Do you need to go and see her again?'

I shook my head. 'I've already lost her, Ness. There's no point going back to see her again.'

'Well, you can always talk to me about her if that helps.'

'Now who's taking on other people's problems?' I said.

'Yeah, but I won't be trying to carry loads on my shoulders like you do. You need to step back a bit Holly, focus on what matters to you, like your future at college and those clothes you're making for the boutique.'

I nodded. 'OK, Major Ness. I hear and obey.'

'And one more thing. Give me your phone, Holly.'

I handed over my phone like a robot, trusting Ness completely.

She dialled my foster sister's number about 10 times. Each time it went to answerphone, so she tried again. Eventually she left a message:

'This is Vanessa, calling you on Holly's phone.' Ness was speaking in a very authoritative voice I'd never heard before. 'You don't know me but I'm very concerned about Holly. Leaving her to care for your little girl is completely unacceptable. She's cracking up here and you know her mum is really ill. Everyone has their problems and yours are no different to anyone else's. I've told Holly that if you aren't back by tonight then I personally am going to call social services and tell them what's going on. If you don't want to lose your child, I suggest you get home as fast as you can.'

'Wow,' I said, as Ness handed back my phone. 'But you wouldn't really, would you? Call social services?'

Ness shrugged. 'I don't know, honestly. At the end of the day you have to think about what's best for the child, don't you?

That little girl is helpless and Lucy is an adult, even if she doesn't behave like one.'

'And don't feel so sorry for her, Holly,' Ness continued. 'You know as well as I do that lots of people struggle with problems in their lives and still look after their children. Lucy has great parents and a great home, and friends like you. She's had a tough time but... There are plenty of single mums out there who have nobody behind them, and they're also having to struggle to make ends meet and they're studying for jobs and stuff. Mum sees them all the time at her night classes.'

'Yeah, but Lucy has always been a bit wrapped in cotton wool, so it's harder for her to be strong,' I said. I did love Lucy. She's been my best friend for years and not even Ness got to disrespect her. 'She's been a brilliant mum till she met this guy. I honestly think she's cracking up inside.'

'Fair enough,' Ness said. 'I'm not trying to judge her, Holly. That's not my place and everybody has a different breaking point. But as your friend, I think it's time she focused a bit more on other people, like her child and her parents and you.'

I was snivelling into Ness's shoulder when I realised Tol was standing there, looking down at me. He had a really concerned look on his face.

'Oh Holly,' he said. 'You're such a strong person. Why is life always throwing so much crap at you?'

And he held out a hand to me and I held it. But not for long coz my common sense soon registered what was going on and I pulled away. 'Have you left Ruby alone?' I demanded.

'It's OK, she's fast asleep on Auntie Marje's lap and Auntie Rhonda changed her nappy and gave her some lovely rice pudding...'

At the end of work I would have got the bus but Tol said that was daft. He insisted that I couldn't carry the baby seat as well as take a buggy. He had a point. He chatted away on the journey home, telling me about some course he's applying to for photo journalism. Not that I really cared about his future, but I let him rabbit on coz I thought it would be too rude to stop him, specially when he was giving me a lift.

'Mum doesn't approve,' he said, negotiating a gritting lorry on the roundabout. 'But what's new?'

'She doesn't approve?' I said. 'But why? I thought she'd be delighted. I thought that's what she always wanted you to do, follow in her footsteps.'

'So did I, but I've realised that nothing I do will ever be good enough for Mum.' Tol sounded really sad, and despite myself, I felt a tiny bit sorry for him.

'She is a bit... harsh,' I said, trying to find the right word.

'Harsh is only half of it!' Tol laughed bitterly. 'Well that's how it seems to me. I feel that she despises me. You met her. What did you think? Am I just being paranoid, Holly?'

What do I say to him? Can you ever say to anyone, 'I think your mum really doesn't love anyone but herself, that she's a cold-hearted creature with very few feelings?'

My mum is no saint but underneath all her strange, screwed-up behaviour me and Ryan knew she really cared for us – really loved us in her own way. My mum cried her eyes out when we got taken into care and she always wanted us back, even if she couldn't always manage to look after us. Would Christiane bother that much about her son if he was taken away from her? Or would she decide this freed her up to go and do some social justice stuff in the world, where she didn't have to care about individual people?

'I don't think she's someone who shows her feelings,' I said, treading very warily.

'If she actually has any feelings in the first place,' Tol said. 'But hey, I'm sorry. You have enough to think about without me droning on about my mum. How's your mum by the way?'

So I told him about how I couldn't get my head round the fact that my mum wanted so badly to die. That she'd probably die any day now. Yeah, I know it's strange I told him all that stuff, but I was following Ness's advice. I was carrying too much on my shoulders and it helped to let it out, let someone else carry a bit for me.

'And you don't want to see her again?' Tol asked me seriously.

I shook my head. 'No – at least I don't think so. I had a present for her but I never gave it to her,' and suddenly the thought of that hurt so much that I couldn't say any more.

'What about if I take you to the hospital, and you give it to her? Tol said when I finally pulled myself together.

'Thanks, but anyway, Martin or Jane can take me when they get back...' but as I said it I realised this wasn't very fair on them. Christmas was going to be hectic, with J and M and the kids not getting back till the night before Christmas Eve, and then Rob and his family arriving the next day.

'Well, think about it,' Tol said, and then Ruby woke up whimpering and I needed to wave some toys to distract her, only she threw back her head and howled in a really heartbroken way.

'She needs her mum, poor little thing,' Tol said.

'Don't we all,' I replied. But he was right. A toddler really really really needs her mum.

'So that friend of yours from the garden centre is coming over tomorrow?' Tol asked, as he helped me into the house with Ruby.

'Yeah, she's going to look after Ruby – if Lucy doesn't show in the meantime, that is,' I told him. 'But thanks very much. I did appreciate your help today.'

'I guess you won't be needing me any more,' Tol sounded really sad.

I said I wouldn't and thanked him for his help but as he was about to drive off, I had a second thought. He pulled on the brake as he heard me tapping furiously on the car window.

'Take me to see my mum – tomorrow. After I finish work in the boutique,' I said to him and he nodded.

'Text me the hospital address,' he said. 'And your address at work and when you want me to collect you. And Holly, take care of yourself. Don't let Lucy off the hook too quickly. Even if she comes back tonight, she's got to learn.'

'Don't worry,' I assured him. 'I intend to give her a proper roasting.'

The supplies I had for Ruby were running low. It was all very well Lucy just leaving a pile of nappies and a couple of outfits in my bedroom. Ruby had lost a mitten today and I was sure she had some thicker socks among all those clothes Lucy kept in the chest of drawers. So I left Ruby in her playpen and went to explore.

I wasn't surprised that the door to Lucy's flat was locked. I sort of knew it would be. But I was sick of this game playing. I guessed I would find a spare key with the others in Jane's bedroom and sure enough, there it was. It even had a label on it to make my life easy.

I felt really bad opening the door to Lucy's flat because I knew she didn't want me to be there. And I very quickly found out why. There were two empty bottles of Jack Daniels in the bin and a half-empty bottle in the fridge. And a bottle of Baileys and a bottle of rosé wine and some of those brightly coloured things that taste like nail varnish, and by Lucy's bed there was an almost empty bottle of vodka. I found another empty bottle of Baileys in the bin there and when I did a thorough search of the kitchen I discovered a bag stuffed under the sink. There must have been six empty wine bottles in there and several bottles of spirits.

Jane had been right to be worried. My guess was that Lucy had probably started helping herself to a glass at night coz it helped her to sleep, and one or two glasses had turned into three or four. And then she'd met this guy and it looked like he'd been encouraging her to drink. I don't think vodka has ever been Lucy's style and I put that down to him.

Anyway, I was going to follow Ness's advice and not start getting too involved in someone else's problems, even if she was my BF. I had my own future to focus on and a girl has only so much energy to go round. I would talk to J and M as soon as they came back – whether or not Lucy turned up in the meantime.

At least Keesh sounds like she's in a really good place. She sent me some pictures from the monastery which was built in the 16th century or some time like that. It's dead dramatic and beautiful, especially in the snow. She says she's sleeping in a turret and sharing a room with a lovely woman who spent the last year travelling round India with a yoga mat. This woman's younger brother is also staying there. Keesh says he's quite "easy on the eye". Apparently everyone at the monastery is very open minded and they welcome people from all kinds of faiths and backgrounds. She says she still feels a tiny bit panicky sometimes but the people around her are so kind. Also the minister is even more chilled and fun than she'd realised and she's looking forward to spending Christmas with her and her family.

I fed Ruby and bathed her and finally managed to get her to settle. I brought her cot down and put it in my room and I also found the baby monitor. I could hear her snuffling gently as I got myself some supper. I half wish I'd let Tol buy me that takeaway he offered, coz I'm pooped and don't have the energy for anything fancy. I managed to heat beans, which I had with some of the sausage rolls Jane had left in the fridge. And I had crisps and a bit of that choccie Christmas log. I think I'd earned it. I got out a bottle of wine but put it away again. I wasn't really in the mood after finding Lucy's stash.

OK, enough now. Just going to catch the news before I turn in for the night. Night night, Diary.

Middle of the night – 2am

I'm wide awake and my heart is racing. I shouldn't have watched
the news. There's no reason that the girl's body they found in the
canal is Lucy's. There are thousands, probably millions of blonde
girls in their late teens in this country. And it's not like it was
actually in Corrington. Haylinge is about 20 miles away and there's
no reason Lucy would go there. I keep telling myself that over and
over and over. But I've just got this really bad feeling in my gut that
it is her. I kind of know it is her. No, that's stupid. It doesn't have to
be her. What would she be doing there? And who would kill her?
She's just gone on some partying spree with this Aiden guy and
she's probably sound asleep in his bed just now.

They don't say on the news if this girl has been killed or if it's
some horrible drowning accident or whatever. They just want
people to call in if they know someone who is missing. So do I call,
or don't I? Calling in doesn't mean I'm admitting that it could be
her, does it?

I rang Dan after I saw the story but he wasn't picking up. I
texted him to say I was being daft but I was really scared about
Lucy. He texted back to say he understood but I really shouldn't
worry, there was no reason why it had to be her. He sent me a
big hug and promised he'd ring me tomorrow. (Poor bloke, I can
tell he's cut up badly about Rani and trying to be brave.) I texted
Ness, too, and she said I should try not to fret. She'll be over early
tomorrow to mind Ruby and she's sure that Lucy is fine because
as I pointed out, the body was found in Haylinge, which isn't
Corrington or London. And there must be thousands of blonde girls
out partying in pink glittery frocks on a winter's night. I didn't know
the bit about the pink frock. That must have been on a later report
that I missed. Oh God, that just made it worse, coz I bet Lucy took
her sparkly pink frock with her. I've made myself not go up and
see if it's missing from her wardrobe coz if it is that will just make

things even worse.

I sent Sean an email somewhere around midnight. I told him that I knew I was being stupid but I was so worried coz I had this gut feeling. Then I said that I knew that a gut feeling doesn't mean anything when you're panicking because it's just the panic that makes you think like that. I've been checking to see if he's replied but nothing yet. I know it's early morning there and he mentioned they were having some kind of party thing, so he probably won't get my message for ages.

More than anything I want to text or call J and M and say I don't know where Lucy is and a girl got killed, but how horrible would that be for them? I don't know anything for sure and I'd just ruin the last day of their holiday. They'd be hanging round the airport and sitting on the plane going frantic with worry and that would be just horrific for them. And anyway by tonight, when they get home, Lucy will probably be here safe and sound. Or if she isn't... Well, we deal with that when we know something definite.

I've also tried Lucy's phone a thousand times, or so it feels. But her inbox is now full and she's not answering. I have left her loads of messages so that could be the reason.

I wish I'd written down that police number they put on the screen. I suppose I could look it up on the internet. But if I look it up I'm admitting that it could be Lucy. But I've got to do something!!

About 5am

I rang the police helpline. It took a while to get through. They said they'd had lots of calls. But they took me seriously and they recorded Lucy's description. They said they don't have many details yet but they could tell me that the girl's body was found about 10pm last evening and she'd only been in the water about half an hour. And there were lots of parents and friends and relatives reporting girls who hadn't come home from going out partying. They wouldn't tell me much else but they asked me details, like her age, the colour of her eyes, whether she had any scars or distinguishing features. I said to the woman on the phone that I knew it probably wasn't Lucy coz Lucy was probably in London, and she didn't say anything. But that doesn't mean anything either. I think they're trained not to give anything away. The woman just said they would be in touch if my description matched the dead girl's. I gave them all the contact details I could think of.

This was probably the worst night of my life. I really needed to talk to someone. I felt guilty about ringing Ness coz she's been so brilliant and I think Dan thinks I'm over-reacting. I didn't want to ruin the night of some innocent person who needs their sleep, so I rang Tol. He answered all bleary but said it was OK. He understood. He asked if I needed him to come over, but I said it was alright. I just needed to talk to someone and he said that was fine.

So we talked for a couple of hours. I talked and talked about how worried I am about Lucy but after a while I needed to talk about other stuff. I asked him what he was thinking of that night he walked out on me, not knowing if my brother was alive or dead. He said, 'Do you want the truth?' and I said yes, I needed to hear it. And he said he was convinced he'd killed my brother and he was frightened witless, and all he could think of was that he needed to kill himself because he couldn't live with that guilt.

'And I couldn't think about you or what you were going through coz I knew you'd hate me... But I didn't mean to desert you Hols. You must've thought I just ran away, but I thought I was doing the right thing. In some twisted warped way, I really believed it was best if I just got out of your life and did away with myself.'

'Yeah, that is kind of hard to believe,' I said. 'From where I stood it seemed cowardly. Really cowardly.'

'I can understand that.'

'So why didn't you?' I asked, amazed at how cold I sounded.

'Good question. Actually I rang the hospital coz I had to know, and I heard that he was doing OK, so I rang my cousin in Normandy and said I needed to come over. We were a bit like brothers when we were little as we spent so much time together and he kind of always looks out for me. He's like in his late 20s and he's this advertising executive, but he's had some drug problems himself and his parents are... they're a lot more understanding than mine. He transferred some money into my account and I got the ferry over to France. He made me sign into this rehab programme, which he paid for himself, and I've been clean ever since.'

'So you say.'

'My parents sold their London place coz my dad retired and moved up this way full time, and so I was a bit freaked about moving back to live with them. At first I was worried I'd run into you but kind of always hoping I would, so I could explain.'

'Yeah, but you didn't exactly come looking for me, did you?' I insisted, not wanting to let him off the hook. 'It was just coincidence that we saw each other in the garden centre.'

'There's no such thing as coincidence,' Tol said mysteriously. 'OK, I take that back. It was coincidence that Mum and Dad picked you up that night you nearly got run over. I don't want you thinking I staged some near-death experience just to get you under our roof!'

'So you tracked me down? Like some kind of stalker?' I was amazed and a bit shocked.

'You could say that,' Tol said. 'Yeah, I was looking for you, Holly, coz I knew I had to apologise and I thought it was better to kind of casually bump into you at work than turn up at your college or something... So I persuaded my parents your garden centre was way better than the one they used to go to!'

'But how did you? I mean, how did you know where I worked?

Where I went to college?' This was really creepy.

'You're on Facebook aren't you? And that guy you friended from France... coz he said he liked your artwork that some friend of his reposted... that's my cousin.'

That will teach me to be so vain! When this rather fit looking French guy sent me a friend request with a message saying some mate of his had shown him some of my "amazing" artwork, I'd not hesitated to accept the request.

'Ah,' I said. Coz what else can you say to something like that?

Then I asked him something I really wanted to know. 'When you thought about killing yourself, what made you want to go on living?'

'Because I knew your brother was going to be OK... because, well because I thought maybe I could become a better person, because I thought maybe... Oh, I don't know what to call it.'

'Hope,' I said. 'I think that's the word you're looking for. And that's what my mum has lost but my brother can maybe still find.'

'Tell me about it,' Tol said gently. And I did because I knew there was no way I'd be able to sleep till I knew whether or not Lucy was that girl in the canal.

FRIDAY 23 DECEMBER

I went into the boutique coz I thought I'd go crazy if I stayed at J and M's fretting and worrying. Ness was at the house with Ruby and I knew she'd be very capable. She told me that Bea has a five-year-old son and she's used to looking after him. Now there's another piece of information I wasn't expecting.

Davina instantly knew that something was wrong and she was very kind. She could hardly miss my deathly complexion and those huge bags under my eyes. So I told her what had happened. She said I was brave to come into work when I had so much on my mind. I said I would never let her down and she said I was 'bloody brilliant'. That's a huge compliment from Davina and it meant a lot to me. But she also said I should go home if I wanted to. I said I'd rather stay, so Davina set to work on doing my make-up. 'I'm slapping it on thick, daahling, like we used to have it for photo shoots. Don't want the customers thinking I'm employing members of the undead.'

Davina also insisted that I left my phone on (normally a total no-no in the boutique) in case anyone was trying to phone me. So I picked up immediately when the police rang. 'Is that Holly

Richards?' the WPC asked. 'Are you somewhere with friends or somewhere you can sit down? I'm afraid I have some rather bad news for you.'

But what is bad news? It's all relative really. There was something weirdly reassuring in hearing this particular news, coz the first thing I thought after they told me was 'Lightning doesn't strike twice... definitely not on the same day! So Lucy can't be the girl in the canal.'

It's not that I wanted Mum to die, or that I'm happy about it in any way, but Mum had given up the will to live and Lucy still has so much to live for.

Mum didn't die naturally. She made the decision herself. Somehow she got the strength to get out of her room and slip out of the security door, and she managed to get out onto the roof. Then... I don't really like to think about that. The first thing I asked the policewoman was who would plan the funeral and she said I shouldn't worry about that just yet. There would have to be a coroner's examination and an inquest. And the hospital had staff who would help me with the funeral. They were used to dealing with patients who have no relatives or very few, the WPC told me, and I wouldn't have to identify the body because the hospital staff would do that. Like this was meant to comfort me in some way.

The first thing I thought about when I ended the call was that Mum would never get that present I'd bought her. I very calmly texted Tol to say thank you but he didn't need to take me to the hospital coz Mum had died.

Davina closed the boutique and drove me home herself. She even ushered some customers out of the shop, explaining there had been a family crisis and she had to shut early. She's a good woman Davina, whatever anyone says. She even came in for a bit and made sure I was OK. Ness was there and she had the kettle on ready coz I'd texted ahead to tell her the news. It didn't feel quite real to me, but there was a voice going round and round in my head saying, 'Lucy is going to be alright'. And somehow I knew that was true, coz the feeling of dread I'd had all night had lifted. J and M would be home soon, and Lucy would be there before they arrived. And everyone would live happily ever after and my mum would no longer be living in terror.

Actually it didn't work out quite like that. Martin and Jane and the boys came back about 9pm and Lucy still wasn't home.

I can't write any more, Diary, coz it's really late and I'm so knackered, and kind of shellshocked and sad. I think I'm going to fall asleep here and now. I'll tell you the rest tomorrow.

SATURDAY 24 DECEMBER
– Christmas Eve

11 am-ish

I'm having a lie-in. Jane says I deserve it. She says she thinks I ought to take it easy for the rest of Christmas and New Year and she will look after me but I said, no, I have work to go to, and a costume to finish for Davina's ball.

I had a long chat with Jane last night. I let them get in through the door first, and Ness made them tea while I listened to Ryan's description of how lame the journey home had been and let Simon show me the brochure with the skating dinosaurs in it (which was the same one he'd had on his bedroom wall before they went away). And Simon had brought me back a plastic dinosaur he'd selected especially for me, and Ryan had brought me this toy reindeer which you squeezed and choccie reindeer poos came out of one end... And Martin told me that he and Ryan had decided they wanted a husky and Jane laughed and said that she'd have to see about that...

The first moment I could I told Jane that I needed to speak to her – in private. So while Martin put Si to bed and attempted to persuade Ryan that he didn't need to stay up till after midnight,

Jane and I went and sat in her little office and drank some of the Baileys they'd brought back for me. I told her everything that had happened since she'd been away, except I was really careful about how I did it, so she would know that there was nothing to panic about.

Jane was brilliant. Well, just her normal self really. I could see she was worried about Lucy but she let me tell her all the details without getting hysterical like some parents would. I guess maybe when you've dealt with kids who set fire to the beds when other kids are sleeping in them, you can cope with most things! She said she was incredibly sorry I'd been left to deal with all the problems and when Lucy turned up (coz Jane seemed very confident that she would) she was going to make sure she realised how much worry and trouble she'd put me through. She said she would also be having a very serious talk with Lucy about whether she was really up to coping with a child all by herself. Maybe it was time Lucy started to think about going to college and letting Jane share some of the child care so Lucy could have some time to herself. But first and foremost, she needed a bit of help with the alcohol problem.

I told Jane about my mum and she said that was terrible and why hadn't I told her that first. She gave me a long hug. I said that my mum was dead and probably at peace and Lucy was alive and more of a priority, and Jane said she could sort of understand my logic. She assured me she'd help me in any way she could with the funeral and with anything else I needed, and break the news to Ryan if I'd like that... and I said, yes please, because I didn't feel I could cope with anything else. To be honest, I was dead worried about how the news about Mum would affect Ryan.

Then because we were talking about Ryan I told Jane about him cutting himself with the knife, and how terrified I'd been that he would really harm himself. Jane wasn't as shocked as I'd imagined.

'It's rare among boys, but not that rare,' she told me. 'According to research, boys are more likely to drink or take drugs or get into fights rather than cutting themselves, but your brother is quite a sensitive soul, and he's been through a lot. But poor you, Holly, worrying about him wandering off into the snow. That must have been awful for you.'

Jane said she understood why I hadn't told her before but I mustn't worry any more. She would make sure that Ryan got the help he needed.

'Will you confront him about the cutting? Tell him he must stop?' I asked her. 'I'm not sure if...'

Jane shook her head, smiling. 'No. As I'm sure you were about to say, that wouldn't really help. He's cutting himself for a reason. I suspect because there's so much mixed-up feeling inside him. I think he's really scared because he doesn't know where he belongs in the world and that terrifies – and hurts – him really badly. The cutting helps him express that pain. We all need to focus on making him feel that he's here for good, that we will stick with him through thick and thin. That we're never giving up on him.'

'Yes, but will he believe that?' I asked Jane, hoping what she said would be possible, but not feeling at all confident.

'Martin and I talked about it when we were away. We talked about all the ways we can make Ryan feel he's not going to be leaving us. And that's going to be even more important now that your mother...' Jane's words trailed off, and I could tell she was swallowing tears. That really moved me... that she cared about Mum so much. I had to stop from breaking down; there would be time for tears later but just now there were things I needed to talk to her about.

'Yeah, I think anything that makes Ryan feel he belongs here, that he's settled and really cared for will help,' I told Jane.

'And he is, he really is,' Jane said, her eyes still wet with tears.

'We were watching the boys watching the dino show for the umpteenth time, and Martin became really emotional – you know what he's like, Holly. He said to me that he loves Ryan and Simon so much, that he sees them the same as his own sons. That he feels he has four sons and two daughters. One of those daughters is you, you know, Holly.'

And then I really had to cry, and Jane and me had a long hug. But then something occurred to me.

'Ryan watched the dino show?' I asked surprised. 'I thought he'd think it was really babyish.'

'Well, we did wonder, but Ryan really started to relax when he was away. He was like a child, quite a young child, once he got past the trying to be cool and showing off,' Jane explained. 'We have great photos to show you of Ryan and Si playing in the snow together, Ryan and Si queuing up to visit Santa's grotto, going on the husky sledge and the toboggan ride, petting the reindeers and woolly ponies... Of course, Ryan convinced himself he was doing all these things to make sure Si was OK, but it really amazed us how well they got on. Ryan even told some boys that were having a bit of a laugh at Simon that Si was his "little brother" and nobody laughed at his brother – which is definitely a first.'

That was brilliant to hear. My brother has had such a downer on Simon since the adoption order went through; he'd really resented him. I don't imagine it will all be hunky dory from here on, but this was a good start.

'And Martin has promised Ryan a dog, a family-friendly dog but a dog which will be first and foremost his; which he can choose and name, and which will be encouraged to sleep in his room because apparently that's essential – according to Martin, who appears to be the expert on this subject – but which no doubt me and Martin will end up walking much of the time. At the moment the dog of choice is a husky but I think we may be able to persuade him to look closer to home!'

That was also good news, something of his own to really care for. I think that will do Ryan good.

'But how do you think he will react to the news of Mum's death?' I asked Jane. 'I kind of worry he will pretend it doesn't matter and sort of bury it all inside him, and then it will come out in some other way. Maybe cutting himself?'

'Yes, that occurs to me too, but we have no way of knowing. We can only wait and see, and keep a close eye on him, and give him all the support and reassurance we can.'

8pm

Actually Ryan howled with grief when Jane told him and clung to her, and to me, like he was a toddler. Between us Jane and I rocked him in our arms and smoothed his hair, and we told him that it was OK, and that we loved him and that we would always love him. And Ryan even let Simon give him a dinosaur to hold, coz that was Si's way of showing he cared.

Jane told him to take his time and think about how he wanted to remember Mum, whether he wanted to come to the funeral or do something of his own. Ryan said he thought he might write a poem for Mum, but he needed to think about it.

I realise I haven't written anything about Lucy yet and there's a reason for this. Lucy did turn up some time in the middle of last night and I heard her burst into tears as Martin opened the door to let her in. Today Lucy is really angry with me coz she knows I've told Jane everything. But honestly, was she hoping she could just slink in with a black eye and nobody was going to make any kind of fuss? And the most important thing here is Ruby. It wouldn't be fair to Ruby to just brush everything under the carpet.

This afternoon I did a quick whizz round the shops. Davina stuffed some 20 pound notes into my hand when she left yesterday and said she'd pay me properly in the new year. That was dead nice of her coz she was giving me her own money, not money out of the boutique accounts. But I was careful about what I spent it on because after all it's the thought that counts. Most important is having enough to feed me and Keesh and pay our rent, at least for a few months in the new year. What happens after that is anyone's guess but I have this feeling we will probably be OK. Keesh is a fighter and a very good saleswoman and I think Davina is keen to have her back. Talking of which, I got a text from Keesh saying she's having a good time with her minister and the family. She says it's absolute chaos in that household coz the pastor has twin girls of 10 who fight all the time, but that makes it almost restful going out to work at the Christmas project for homeless people. I said I hoped Keesh wasn't overdoing things but she said she feels stronger inside and not so anxious any more. She's been talking a lot about Nathan to people on the retreat and now she wants to focus on something else. She has some new ideas for clothes she wants to make for herself, and she wants to talk to Davina about a theme for the windows for the New Year's sale.

Keesh says she's had a few texts from the guy at the retreat. The one whose sister she shared a room with. She says he's really cool and has travelled all over the world. However, he's never been to Corrington and he says it's probably time he came up here, coz he hears it has a terrible football team and he needs to see it for himself! So Keesh has said he's welcome to come and stay with us when he does ☺.

J and M's eldest son, Rob and Mrs Rob (her real name is Carol but it's a family joke coz one of our foster kids got a bit mixed up and the name kind of stuck) and the three boys arrived this afternoon, and the house became completely crazy for a bit. The boys always want to play with Ruby and Si gets a bit frantic, and what with the excitement of Christmas Day tomorrow, it was a total madhouse. So I've snuck up here to wrap some presents and to make that dinosaur for Si. Lucky I'm now so quick at making stuff and lucky that Jane has such a cool sewing machine. I found just the right material on a market stall today and I already had the shape worked out in my head, so it didn't take long to draw and cut out the pattern. I don't know what kind of dinosaur it is but it's based on the one that Si carries round with him most of the time. I nearly took a short cut and got some stick-on eyes but then I remembered that Ruby is just the age when she will put anything in her mouth if it's left lying around. And so I got some sew-on ones that took longer.

It's good, too, that I can cry while I'm stitching. Martin came up to see me and bring me trifle and a glass of sherry. I hate both but I didn't tell him. He asked if I was doing OK and I said sure, and he showed me some of the photos on his phone of the huskies and my brothers patting a reindeer. No, that isn't a mistake Diary, I did write "brothers".

He also told me that Ryan got a call this afternoon from Susanna. She's asked if he wants to meet up in the new year and there's some date arranged for this. 'But what was great was that Ryan told her about your mum and the funeral – and he cried when he told her – and then he asked if she'd come along. Apparently she said that of course she would.'

I could go downstairs if I really wanted to but I'm going to send an email first. I felt I needed a little treat so I just opened Sean's present and it's a pendant, with delicate patterns painted on glass. It's very pretty but not quite my normal style. But I will wear it every day from now on. I'm going to email and tell him that I love it, and that I love him. I should tell him about Mum but I don't want to do that tonight, by text. I want to wait till I can tell him properly by phone.

Later

Guess what I just found! It's an email from that snotty secretary, except she's not quite as snotty as I thought. She says that she had been thinking about my message and she remembered that there used to be another John Richards in the company, who was definitely from England (her boss is originally from Scotland, but Americans often think everyone who comes from the UK is "English") but the properly English guy moved on to one of their rival companies about two years ago. She knew that one of the other secretaries in the New York office was friends with his wife and she's sent her an email and hopefully she will get back to her after Christmas. She can't promise anything but she hoped it might help me, and she wished me a "Happy Holiday"!

Will wonders never cease! I'd have sworn that woman had a lump of iron where her heart should be ☺.

And Sean has emailed back to say he's sorry my present is only little and if he could he would buy me the most precious stones in the world, but even those wouldn't be as beautiful as me! I think he was a bit tipsy when he wrote that but it's still cute. He tells me that his mum is a bit upset because her sore spot has got quite a bit puffier and the local hospital says she mustn't worry about it too much coz the operation is booked for as soon as she's back in England, but of course she is, although she's trying really hard not to spoil anyone's holiday. That makes me feel a bit awful for being such a cow about her.

I think I might just go downstairs in my PJs for a bit and see whether any of the kids have exploded with excitement yet.

7am

I just had the strangest dream that me and Ryan were little kids and Mum was trying to give us a good time, and we woke up to find stockings at the end of our beds. But when we opened the stockings there were lots of tiny bits of cogs and springs and things that you find inside all kinds of electrical stuff. And Mum came into our bedroom and she was crying and saying that the remote control for the telly wasn't working because "They" had decided that someone was sending her messages through the telly and they had to stop her getting them. So we couldn't watch any of the Christmas specials or the Queen's speech or anything, but I told her that wasn't really true because the telly still worked if you pressed some buttons on the side of it, even if you couldn't get some of the satellite channels.

But Mum still went on crying and said that maybe now they had control of the remote they could control everything in her life. And she got scared that they were going to rewind her life and make her go back to when... And she started shaking and couldn't say what it was she was frightened of. But I told Mum that you can't rewind people's lives. The past is the past, and the only thing you can think about is what's happening now, and what might happen in the future. She said, what if they fast forwarded her life and I said I didn't think that could happen either. But I said sometimes we just have to accept that we can't be in control of everything, and it doesn't matter if we can't see all the stations coz we can't control everything in the world... just make the best of what we have. Then I realised that Mum wasn't there any more because I remembered that she'd already switched herself off, so I took Ryan's hand and we walked out of the room and next door to a room where J and M had proper stockings waiting for us.

Now I'm awake I can see that "Santa" has been coz there is a bulgy stuffed sock at the end of my bed (looks like one of Martin's). Good old Jane. I know she's made stockings for everyone in the house: Rob and Mrs Rob and their kids, and Ryan and Si and Lucy and Ruby, and Martin. I bet even Boots and the rabbits have mini-stockings somewhere with little treats inside them and Martin will have made a very big stocking for Jane with loads of her favourite things inside, coz he likes to spoil her sometimes. And she definitely deserves it.

Now I'm going to snuggle down to sleep coz I'm feeling a bit knackered and a bit headachy. And I've got to be fully fit to enjoy my Christmas dinner! No more crazy dreams now. I want to dream about Christmas card scenes with perfect fluffy white snow and hot chocolate and chestnuts and throwing snowballs at the guy I love...

10.30pm

When I was a kid the end of Christmas Day always felt a bit sad to me. I'd be sad coz it was over but also because somehow Christmas is never as good as you think it's going to be. But this year was so strange because of Mum dying and all the stuff that's been going on recently with Ryan and Keesh and Lucy and all that...

So I just decided I was going to let the day carry me along and live each minute as it happened. I promised myself that I wasn't going to try too hard to put a brave face on things because I wanted to show my brother that it's totally OK to let your feelings out.

As it turned out it was probably one of the best Christmas Days ever. Sure, I felt very sad but I also felt kind of relieved that all the worst things seemed to be over. And all the adults were so kind and considerate to me and Ryan, checking out if we were OK and giving us space to talk or be on our own. Rob's boys and Si didn't understand any of that and you can't spoil Christmas for little kids, can you? So me and Ryan ended up joining in with some of the fun things too and having quite a good time.

Even Lucy was trying to be nice to me although I could tell she was still angry – maybe feeling a bit betrayed that I'd told Jane the truth about her leaving me to look after Ruby. But honestly, what did she expect? Just coz I'm her BF doesn't mean I'm going to tell lies about her going off and leaving her daughter. I think underneath it all she's terrified that Jane might say she's not able to look after Ruby and insist she goes to rehab or something, coz Lucy knows that her mum would always put a young child's needs first, even if it meant falling out with her own daughter. So Lucy was being extra bright and cheerful and trying to prove she was the best mum ever, fussing over Ruby and making sure she got to experience every tiny bit of Christmas, like the cracker pulling and the turkey carving and the Christmas pud being set alight. She took endless photos of Ruby on her mobile. She even made the poor little mite sit and watch the Queen making her speech. Fortunately Ruby was smart enough to fall asleep.

Si's soft dinosaur was a big success but there was a bit of tension coz Rob's youngest boy wanted to play with it and Si wasn't having any of that. So we had a few tears and plenty of sulking. But what's Christmas without some arguing and crying ☺?

I got a text from Keesh who said her day serving Christmas dinners to homeless people was "amazing". Ness texted to say that her mum and Bea had an argument over the Christmas cake about animal rights, but fortunately they both calmed down and made up afterwards, and anyway her mum was dead smitten by Bea's son so that made everything OK. Dan also texted to say he'd found out from Rani's FB that she was engaged to one of her distant cousins who is a company director, but he didn't care because he was done with crying about her and he was having an OK day with his mum and dad. And there was also a text from Tol to say his mum had chosen Christmas Eve to tell his father she wanted a divorce:

Typical Mum pickin a date like that. But 2 b honst Dad lookd quite relieved. They spent all Xmas lunch makin plans bout how they goin 2 split the money and house up between them. Never seen them get on so well!

Hope u doin OK. Ring me if u need to talk bout your mum. Or anythin elz. Happy Christmas Holly Babe xxx

And Sean rang and I told him about my mum and he said he would come home for the funeral, and I must let him know as soon as there's a definite date. And I said that would be brilliant.

Hey Diary, I think I'm putting the light out really soon. I feel that wiped out. And just a tiny bit sick. Maybe I shouldn't have had that second bit of Chrissie pud.

Oh, one more thing. My brother just knocked on the door to give me his Christmas present which was this dodgy perfume spray he'd picked up on some market stall. But I said it was great and he thanked me for his DVD of ghost stories. He said it was brilliant, but he's probably an even better actor than I am. He even let me give him a little bit of a hug before he pulled away.

SATURDAY 31 DECEMBER
New Year's Eve

Hello Diary, remember me? Well, guess who woke up with a hideous sickness bug on Boxing Day and had to go to bed for days and days? Jane did get her wish to wait on me hand and foot after all. I just wished someone would shoot me for the first two days and then I just slept and slept and slept and slept. Like I was Sleeping Beauty.

I did start worrying, on about day three, about work but Jane said there was nothing to worry about. I couldn't go anywhere near other human beings before I was over the bug thing, so neither Davina or Marje could complain that I was pulling a sickie. And I got a text from Keesh to say she was missing being at work and had asked Davina if she could maybe go in for a half-day, and it went so well she went back the next day as well. And Ness says the garden centre is dead quiet and she's bored stiff clearing out all the dead Christmas trees and holly wreaths and stuff, and she hopes I won't be away too long coz everyone misses me.

A couple of human beings have been in to see me with news from the outside world. Ryan tells me that he's about to get a Leonberger. 'A what?' I said and he told me that they're massive woolly dogs that come from this place called Leonberg in Germany. They're dead gentle and friendly and confident and loyal and they don't drool like most big dogs. Apparently the twins' cousin has this Leonberger but he's found out he's allergic to dogs and his parents need to find a new home for it. Ryan met this dog on Boxing Day and he's made his mind up. J and M have met the dog since and they agree it's huge, but dead soppy. Jane tells me she thinks that having a really big, dead-loyal dog will help Ryan's self-esteem. And I suspect she's pretty smitten with it herself coz she gets this silly grin on her face when she talks about it. What Boots will think is anybody's guess but he's a pretty smart cat and he can take care of himself. And I guess he'll appreciate that this Leo is far too big to sleep on the bed!

Lucy also came to visit me and to apologise big time. She told me she'd been a total idiot and she hoped I could forgive her. She also explained what had happened during the trip to London and it was pretty nasty.

She said that Aiden was getting a bit weird on the drive down, criticising everything she did and telling her what he did and didn't want her doing as his girlfriend. They'd crashed at his sister's house on the first night and that had been OK. The London party had been quite fun, but as the evening went on she started to feel more and more freaked out about the way that Aiden seemed to want to control her every move. She also realised that he was constantly topping up her drinks, but she was still sober enough to know that there was no way she was going to have sex with Aiden's friend just because Aiden said she should. And she put up a fight when Aiden told her she was being a little bitch and smacked her across the face, catching her eye with his ring. He'd then grabbed her by the arm and twisted it, but she'd had the sense to shriek. And some of the other guests had come upstairs to see what all the fuss was about on the landing. Aiden had tried to say that his girlfriend was drunk and he was trying to get her to lie down for a bit but Lucy wasn't having that. She knew that Nathan would never, ever, ever have asked her to sleep with another bloke or do anything she didn't want, so she told the other guests what was going on. Some of the men weren't very sympathetic but a group of girls recognised that Lucy was genuinely scared. They fetched their husbands and boyfriends who told Aiden to back off and between them they looked after Lucy and took her to the station and lent her the money for her train journey back to Corrington. One of the women even lent her a coat so she wouldn't freeze, coz all her bags were in Aiden's car.

'But he still has a key,' I said, worrying that Lucy hadn't seen the last of him.

'Yeah, but he hasn't,' Lucy told me. 'I took it back on the way down in the car, when I was starting to feel a bit spooked by him. He'd been having a go at me about how I needed to change my hair. Then he told me to get him some gum out of his jacket and I found the key in the pocket. I put it back in my bag and he didn't see. I guess I was picking up on a bad vibe...'

Pity it wasn't sooner, I thought, but at least she's home and safe, unlike that poor girl who drowned in the canal at Haylinge. It seems she was only 16. She was called Hannah, and she'd been out celebrating her friend's 17th birthday. They'd started partying really early in the evening. Her crying mum said on the news that she wasn't the sort to get drunk and fall in the water, but how can you tell? The police haven't said anything more since they gave out her name, and it doesn't sound like they're treating it as a murder.

Lucy has promised she's going to get some help for her drinking problem. Yeah, she does seem to realise she has a problem and it's quite brave of her. I guess the shock of what happened in London has made her start to face up to stuff... and she also admits she needs to think about going back to college coz she's been going a bit crazy spending too much time in the flat. And she's also going to ask her mum if she can help out a bit with child care. You have to take your hat off to Jane – she can make anyone believe that something is their own idea!

Lucy has been helping me finish off the costumes for the masked ball. It's been fun to work on something together, and watch crap TV and gossip about celebrities and fashion and other mindless stuff. And eat ice cream and chocolates (which I've finally got my appetite back for), just like we used to, back in the day. Lucy also says she's definitely coming to Mum's funeral with me and Ryan, and that feels good too.

I'm quite excited about the ball now. I really didn't think I'd ever feel well enough to get out of bed again. Now I'm feeling good to be alive.

Anyway, I need to stop writing you now, Diary, and get ready coz my date will be here in an hour and I don't want to keep him waiting.

SUNDAY 1 JANUARY
A new year!

The ball was just fab like I knew it would be. Davina had hired
the ballroom at the Regal, which is probably the poshest hotel in
Corrington. It has these massive chandeliers and there's a little
balcony where a mini-orchestra was playing, and the tables were
beautiful with all that sparkling silver and the most fantastic flower
arrangements. Everyone had dressed up for the occasion and there
were incredible costumes. Somebody had even come as Marie
Antoinette and had this massive dress over a hooped petticoat that
made it stand out a few feet away from her body, and she wore a
huge powdered wig. And there was a man dressed as a peacock
wearing a very clingy green costume (he had fabulous abs so it
looked good) and a brilliant multi-coloured tail. And there were
several King Charles IIs looking dashing in wide-brimmed hats and
silk coats with big floppy sleeves, and a woman who seemed to be
wearing nothing at all but a lot of body paint and a very confident
smile... and a pantomime horse and a Puss in Boots. Everyone
carried masks but as the evening went on people started to put
them down and lose them and after a while nobody was worrying
about them any more.

Davina was utterly gorgeous in this shimmering coral-blue beaded 1920s dress, with a feathered band around her bobbed hair. Michael was there looking a bit wimpy and had come as a 1920s man who had dressed in a hurry and looked a bit uncomfortable in the linen suit and trousers his partner had carefully picked out for him ☺. And Keesh did come along for a little while dressed as... well, dressed in one of her own creations which was quite low at the front and back and had all the older men nearly passing out with joy. When someone asked her who she'd come as, she said Cleopatra and everyone said that was just right.

Lucy and Dan looked fab as well. There hadn't been a lot of time to make their costumes so I'd gone for a Disney prince and princess look, adapting an old blue evening dress of Jane's and we'd spent hours twisting Lucy's hair into blonde curls. Her eye was still a bit swollen so she kept her mask on most of the evening. I'd made Dan this tunic out of some red velvet material Jane had once bought for making cushions, but never used, and he rented a floppy hat with feathers from the local costume hire shop. He refused to wear tights but he agreed to borrow some leather trousers from his mate, and I think Lucy was impressed by how good his legs looked in them. They made a handsome couple and they seemed to be laughing a lot and having some fun, so who knows? They may start dating eventually. For now they're "just good friends".

And me and my partner? Well I was a sort of highwaywoman in a black bodiced dress that swished as I walked and my partner was all in black as the highwayman himself. And we looked very cool and very stylish. Lucy had done my hair using this hairpiece of Keesh's that cascaded in ringlets down my back, and Jane lent me a dramatic diamond-shaped necklace and some fab drop earrings, all made out of black jet. And the highwayman had his hair swept back in a black velvet bow.

At midnight all the guests stood in a circle and sang Auld Lang Syne, and everyone kissed, as they always do. After Tol kissed me lightly on the lips, he said, 'Happy New Year, Holly, and may the new year be a much better one for you.' And I squeezed his hand and thanked him for being such a good friend, and I left him dancing with the very stunning Carly, who used to be Davina's assistant and is probably the most beautiful girl you could ever imagine. Tol certainly seemed to think so.

I went outside to try and get a signal, and a bit of peace and quiet. 'Sorry to ring at this time, I know you won't have been in bed for very long,' I said to Sean when he answered. 'But I just had to wish you Happy New Year... Give my regards to your mum and dad by the way. Did they enjoy their New Year's Eve?'

'Yeah, I think they managed to enjoy themselves, Mum's met this woman from Yorkshire who's staying at our resort. Apparently she had breast cancer but seems to have made a great recovery, so that's cheered Mum up quite a bit.'

I said this was good and I realised I actually meant it.

'But I miss you Holly, I miss you so much,' Sean said suddenly, his voice all intense and loving. And my knees felt really weak. 'You've been through such a rough time recently and I wish I could've been there for you.'

'I know you do,' I said, and then heard myself say, 'But your mum needed you and you did the right thing to go to Australia with her.'

'Yeah I know, but I also want to be with you, Hols. I want to be there for you always. I think you know that.'

'Always is a long time,' I said, but I was happy he'd said it. 'But I'm pretty tough you know. I'm Holly Richards, don't forget, and I'm good at standing on my own two feet.'

'As if I could,' Sean laughed, at the other side of the world. 'And I wouldn't have you any other way...'